THE PRETTY BOY AND THE TOMBOY

A MÉNAGE ROMANCE

(formerly Deceptive Attraction)

Tara Lain

Tara Lain Books

Copyright

Blurb

Caleb Martin faces a life crisis -- and he's pretty embarrassed about it. A talented soccer star, he has the chance to sign a lucrative five-year contract and be rich and famous. Two problems – Cal's gay and signing the contract means he has to stay in the closet, maybe for life. Plus, he'll have to spend his years diving for soccer balls when he'd like to be helping people like the rest of his family. A one-night stand with a beautiful man rocks Cal, but the mysterious guy vanishes only to reappear where Cal is house-sitting. Too much coincidence? And then a cute tomboy throws Cal's life choices into confusion. How could he wind up with a commitmentphobe and a woman dedicated to her work in Africa? To Top it off, there's a big surprise in a snowstorm. Cosmic joker strikes again.

Dedication

To Buffy Kennedy and all my original 13 members of my Street Team for loving this book in its original version and for all the support and encouragement over the years.

Author's Note

Hi! Thank you for reading *The Pretty Boy and the Tomboy*. This book is a rerelease of one of my earliest bestselling books that was then titled *Deceptive Attraction*. But please note, while I'm known for more than 50 gay romances, **this book is a MMF ménage and includes sex and later love between two men and a woman**. Also, it was written a number of years ago, and hasn't been significantly changed from the original. It was a reader favorite then, and I hope it will be a favorite of yours.

Contents

Chapter One

Sheee-it! Caleb Martin hit the ground, pain flashing through the twice-broken shoulder. Needed breath. More than that, he needed to hang on to the damned soccer ball. *Don't let go.*

He clutched that baby to his chest with his mitts. Pain. All over. *Just your regular. Don't let go.*

Scar tissue held. *Rib broken? Maybe just bruised.*

Had to get up, kick in.

Hands grabbed him and pulled him to his feet. Crap, it hurt. Noise. Crowd cheering. No, more than cheering, going ape shit. The clock must have run out.

Whoa! Two guys grabbed him and hoisted him into the air on their shoulders. He grinned. Brave guys. He was a load. Wobbling. He grabbed one guy's shoulder to stay upright. Hitting the ground again did not sound fun. He waved a mitt to the screaming fans. Oh yeah. Guess he'd blocked the kick that would have tied the game.

Final whistle. Game over. Rocket Dogs win. The season is done. Thank God.

After getting pounded on the back several hundred times, shaking countless hands, giving five media interviews, and taking a quick shower, he stood beside the bench in the locker room trying to get his boxer briefs pulled up.

"Congratulations, Martin."

"Great game, bro."

"Helluva save, baby."

Guys slapped his shoulder in congratulations, and he tried hard not to wince.

Suddenly the noise from the hall got louder. He glanced up to see the locker room door burst open. Well, crap. He pulled the briefs up fast as a wild-eyed girl, probably about nineteen or twenty, ran into the big room. "Cal. Cal, baby."

Her eyes widened when she saw him. Where were his clothes? He grabbed for his shirt as she raced across the open space toward him, bumping into guys in towels and less. A few feet away, she hurled herself straight at his half-naked body. *Think fast, Martin. Catch her, or let her fall? Oof.* The shirt went flying. One hundred twenty pounds of squirming female climbed all over him. He tried to keep her from hurting herself as she grabbed his head, kissing his cheeks, trying to get to his mouth. *Shit.* He twisted his head. *Damn, get this female off!* All around him, he heard the other guys laughing. Fat lot of help they were.

He heard the door open again. Rescue. Two burly guys in security uniforms hurried toward him. Cal grabbed her waist and pushed her toward them, still wriggling. "C'mon, guys, get her off."

The bigger guy, Harry, grabbed her. "Sorry, Cal, she got away from us."

He smiled. "I can see how that could happen."

Harry carried her carefully. *Don't hurt the fans.* She leaned back in Harry's arms and gazed at Cal with puppy-dog eyes. "I love you, Cal."

He laughed. "I love you too."

They dragged her, squirming and yelling, out of the room.

Cal glanced up. His roommate, Lex, stared at him. The guy was grinning, but there was this crease between his eyebrows. Yeah. Cal sighed. Only Lex, the coach, the owner, and one other guy on the team knew that Cal was more interested in the bare asses in the shower than in that cute girl. They were good about it as long as they didn't have to be reminded too often. And that meant Cal got to spend ninety percent of his time pretending to be someone and something he wasn't. Not just pretending to be straight, but also acting like a guy who only wanted to be a huge soccer star in his life. Cal sighed and finished dressing. Man, he was glad the season was over.

* * * * *

Cal pulled his jacket tighter and looked up at the blinking neon sign. Blue Flamingo. Blue Flamingo. Maybe this was the first night of the rest of his life. The night he'd decide to quit hiding and be who he really was. Of course, first he had to be sure he knew who he was.

He glanced again at the sign. It had been a while, but the place still felt pretty homey. He'd had some important moments in this bar. His first dance with a guy. And that amazing night when he'd gotten so drunk and both the gorgeous supermodel, Roan, and Cal's brother Jake had come to rescue him -- right before he came out to his parents. He smiled. Tomorrow he'd see the guys when he went to house-sit for them. Man, that was one house where sitting was a pleasure. But tonight was Blue Flamingo time. If he was gonna make some life decisions, he might as well start in a place where he felt connected. A place where people knew him and valued him as he was. God, he was tired of pretending all the time. Sure, people at the Flamingo knew he was an athlete, but he wasn't really worried about somebody calling the press. He'd been coming here since before he was old enough to drink. The Flamingo was like family.

He jogged the rest of the way across the parking lot and pushed open the door. Heat. Noise. That familiar smell of candle wax and booze, and the pleasant underlying scent of warm men. He pulled off his jacket. *What a crush. Fridays at the Flamingo and the gang's all here.* The men lined up two-deep at the bar, most of the tables were full, and a few guys had already made it to the postage-stamp dance floor.

"Hey, Cal. Long time, no see."

Cal looked up as the cute waiter Hal, who always flirted with him, pushed through the crowd carrying a tray of bottles. "Hey, Hal. How the hell are you?"

"I'm good, handsome. Man, I saw you pull off that save today. You were the hero. Great move."

Cal shrugged. "Thanks. Anybody here I know?"

"Yeah, well most of them probably know you, Mr. Celebrity. But I saw Joe Jack back at your favorite booth, and Peter and a couple of the other guys."

"Thanks. I'll go find them."

"What do you want to drink? I'll bring it when I come back."

"That good Mexican beer." He grinned. "And I'm actually old enough to drink it this time."

"No worries, cutie. I'll see you in a minute."

Hal moved off toward the crowded bar, and Cal surveyed the scene. He towered over most men, so he could make out Joe Jack's shaved skull in the back of the big room. Pressing between the bar crowd and the tables, he headed for the familiar face. As he passed by, a couple of guys reached out with a pat or a fist bump, but in the dim light, he wasn't sure whether he knew them or they just recognized him from the team.

Going toward the booth, he noticed a particularly large group crowded together at the far end of the bar, but they were pressed too close, and he couldn't see what the attraction was. Probably a game of liar's poker. He squeezed between the tables to the booth. "Hey, Joe Jack."

The handsome, rugged face lit up. "Hey, kid. How the hell are you? Man, it's been too long." Joe Jack stood up to give Cal a hug. Though the guy was four or five inches shorter than Cal, the bulk of his biceps and powerful thighs made him someone no guy wanted to mess with. But Cal knew Joe Jack had a seriously gooey center - - if you were brave enough to try to find it.

Cal threw his jacket over the back of the booth as Joe Jack sat down and made space for him. Peter, a good-looking yuppie still in his suit and tie from work, occupied the chair on the outside of the booth. Peter had been his other babysitter on the famous drunken-stupor night. A good guy. "Hey, Peter."

"Good to see you, kid. You've been getting some serious playing time."

"Yeah. The first-string goalie still hasn't been released to play, so Cinderella here gets to go to the ball."

"Not bad exposure for a rookie. That was one hell of a save."

Hal arrived with his beer in time to say, "Yeah, man, you were the MVP. That's gotta mean something serious for next season. I'll bet they start you."

"Thanks, but not likely. I'm still pretty green." Cal could feel some heat in his cheeks. Blushing. The family curse. He wasn't ready to talk about next season. Hell, he wasn't ready to think about it. He'd put that decision off until he was safely alone in the Connecticut house. He pointed toward the bar. "What's the big attraction over at the bar?"

Joe Jack shook his head. "It's a guy. Would you believe it? He's a stranger, and man, is he pretty. I mean girl fucking pretty. He says he's waiting for somebody, but the guys are still buzzing around like some drones at the queen."

"Pretty? You mean like Roan?" Nobody was prettier than his beautiful brother-in-law. Well, more like brother-in-love, since even liberal Connecticut didn't allow three people to marry.

"Kind of, but actually prettier. You know how Roan has that carved kind of face? This guy is softer. Girlier. And he's got blond fucking ringlets, for crap sake."

Cal laughed. "Why aren't you over there contending for the prize, big guy? You love blonds." Joe Jack had been really taken with Cal's brother, Jake.

Joe Jack leaned back. "I haven't entirely ruled it out."

Cal laughed. "Well, I gotta pee anyway, so maybe I'll try to get a look at this paragon."

He slid out of the booth and headed for the men's room. As he passed the bar, he could see four or five guys gathered around someone who was seated. They were leaning in. He craned his neck, but he couldn't see the object of their worship without looking like some groupie. He went into the head, did his business, and returned, hoping to get a better look. Apparently one of the adorers had given up, so Cal slipped into a spot at the back of the group. Being six feet five helped. He peeked over a big brunet's head.

Holy shit.

Joe Jack hadn't been exaggerating a bit. If anything, he'd understated. The guy was looking down at his beer, but Cal still got a good look at the profile. Wheat-colored ringlets stood out from his head, framing a sharp, slightly upturned nose and bright pink cheeks. Not made-up, probably flushed from the heat and attention. Shirley fucking Temple. No, that made him sound cutesy and this guy was not. He was sexy as hell. The man picked up his beer bottle and took a swig. One of the guys near Cal actually sighed. Yeah, who wouldn't want those pretty, pouty lips wrapped around their dick?

And then there was the body. Small, slim, but pure male. The hands around the beer bottle looked rough and calloused, like they'd scrape your butt real nice if he grabbed you. His forearms under the pushed-up sleeves of his blue T-shirt were lean, but ripped and muscled. Shit, what did Jake call Roan? Sex on a stick. No wonder these guys were drooling.

One of the admirers Cal didn't recognize was saying, "C'mon, beautiful. Your boyfriend must've stood you up. Which means he's fucking crazy and doesn't deserve you, so let me buy you a drink, okay?"

Another guy chimed in. "Or me. Am I your type?"

Wow. So with all this adoration, the pretty boy was still buying his own beer.

Ringlets said something, and Cal moved a little closer to try and hear. The man standing in front of him looked up. "Hey, Caleb." He frowned a little, clearly not wanting any more competition. "What are you doing here?"

Yeah, what was he doing there? Eavesdropping? Satisfying his curiosity? Or nurturing the raging hard-on pushing against the zipper of his jeans? The fact was, he hadn't had sex in weeks and hadn't had satisfying sex in -- shit, forever. He wasn't really the bar-pickup type, but the blond was something special.

He started to answer, but suddenly the guy at the bar turned on his bar stool, and Cal got the front-on view for the first time. Holy fucking gorgeous. Cal was staring directly into the tawniest pair of golden eyes, like some kind of cat. Yeah, the cat that ate his voice. He couldn't speak. Just stood there like someone had struck him dumb. The man smiled. Deep dimples appeared in the pink cheeks. That put the finishing touch on the hard-on.

"Caleb." How did he know his name? He must have heard the other guy say it. The blond's voice was soft, a little high, somehow appropriate to his prettiness. He said Cal's name somewhere between a question and a sigh. He looked around at the other men. "You see, I told you I was waiting for someone."

What the f --

Loud protests followed.

"Well, why the hell didn't you say you were waiting for Martin?"

"Some guys have all the luck."

"Hey, Cal, why'd you keep your date waiting, you asshole?"

At a loss was too mild a description. But the guy had things under control. He stepped off the bar stool -- long legs made him a little taller than Cal had guessed, probably about five feet ten -- and extended his hand to Cal. "So now that you've kept me waiting and made me lead on all these handsome guys, I figure it's time you dance with me." The golden eyes stared at Cal as if daring him to deny that they were a couple. Hell, Mrs. Martin didn't raise any dumb sons.

Cal took the man's hand, just as rough as it looked, and after a pause to stare down at the disappointed faces, he pulled the guy toward him, wrapped an arm around his lean shoulders, and turned toward the tiny dance floor. The other men grumbled but backed off. When he and the pretty boy had moved in among the other dancers, Cal turned toward him. Golden eyes gazed up at him. The man held up his arms, ready to let Cal lead. Good. He slipped his arms around the slender body and moved them into a gentle rock. Cal was no great dancer, but fortunately this dance floor didn't allow for much in the way of ballroom style.

They both spoke at the same time. "You want to explain what -
-"

"Thanks for going along --"

The guy smiled up at Cal. "Thank you for going along with me. I was telling the truth; I was supposed to meet a friend here, but he didn't show."

"A friend?"

"Yeah, just a friend."

"Really? Not a lover?"

Cal got an appraising stare. "No. I don't do lovers. It rhymes with commitment."

All righty then. "So your friend…?"

"Yeah. I was planning on killing him the next time I see him for leaving me here alone, but…" He looked at Cal with a soft smile. "I think I changed my mind about that. I'm Elijah, by the way. Eli."

"Caleb. Cal. I guess we'd better not shake hands, or we'll give ourselves away."

"No shaking of hands required." Eli molded his body to Cal's. Cal could feel the man's hard cock pressing against his thigh, and wished for the first time in his very tall life that he was shorter. Man, he would like that hard rod pushing against his cock. Shit, he should run. He could sense this pretty boy was way out of his league in terms of experience, since Cal had only had one committed relationship and a couple of short-term affections. The guy might even be a player, though his reluctance to let his admirers buy him drinks didn't suggest that. But Cal knew he was thoroughly and righteously hooked. He might not have known his type until tonight, but the fact was, Ringlets was his idea of perfect. No, he wasn't going anywhere.

They didn't talk, just moved. Eli's body was hard, but not in a working-out way. More like he used it regularly. Shit, Cal loved the lean, hungry feel of him. He wanted to lift him up so he could wrap his legs around Cal's waist and grind. Oh yeah, that was what he wanted. But even though the Flamingo was a gay bar, it wasn't that liberal, and there was no back room. Cal heard a moan. His? Eli's? He had an uncomfortable feeling --

"Did I just hear you moan, big guy?" The golden eyes were heavy-lidded.

Time to go for it. He hoped his palms weren't sweating since he wasn't really a "big moves" man. Cal leaned down so his lips rested on Eli's ear. The curls tickled his nose. "Just imagining what I'd do to you if there was a back room in this place."

"Hellfire, there's a back room somewhere." Eli's breath was hot. "Take me there. Now."

Oh, Jesus. Had his cock ever been this hard? He had to do this. "There's a motel down the street I've stayed in a couple of times when I had too much to drink. We could go there."

"Sounds positively civilized compared to the parking lot scenario I was picturing. Let's go, baby."

Cal looked up. A dozen pairs of eyes, including Joe Jack's, were glued to him and his pretty partner. He'd take serious ribbing for this. Or maybe they'd cheer, since Joe Jack always told him he needed to get laid more. Did he care? Hell, no. He took Eli by the hand and, both erections on full display in tight jeans, led the man off the dance floor. "You leave anything at the bar? Have a tab?"

"No. Paid as I went."

"Got a coat?"

"On my bike."

Bike? Really? "Let me grab mine from the table."

Still holding Eli's hand, Cal approached the booth where Joe Jack sat. He looked part amused and part envious. Cal was glad he wasn't mad. "Good to see you, Joe Jack."

"So you capture the prize and then carry it away."

"Something like that." Cal grabbed his coat from the back of the booth. "See ya."

"See if I tell you about my fantasies in the future."

Damn. Cal liked the big alpha male. "Sorry."

The man waved a tattooed arm. "Hey, kid, I'm joking. If that pretty boy liked me, I'd've been out of here a half hour ago."

Eli laughed and squeezed Cal's hand.

Cal grinned. "Thanks, buddy. See you soon."

He led Eli toward the door. Ringlets leaned in and raised his head so that Cal could hear. "Thought for a minute there you were going to give me away."

"Not without a fight."

"Oooh, that would have been something to see. You and the tattooed he-man?"

"Yeah, well, Joe Jack's a friend and not someone I'd choose to mess with if I could avoid it."

They'd made it to the entrance and paused for Cal to put on his coat. The teasing left Elijah's face. "Listen. I had a chance to go home with a lot of guys tonight. I chose you. I'm not letting go till we're both so satisfied our lips form a permanent smile."

Ooookay. Time to go.

Outside, the November chill made Cal shiver. Eli must be freezing in his T-shirt. Cal wrapped an arm around him and pulled him close. "Want to get your jacket and take my car?"

"No. Don't like to leave the bike. I'll follow you."

Eli stepped away and walked toward a beautiful red rice crotch rocket parked by the fence. Probably a Japanese model. Hard to tell from a distance, plus Cal was distracted by Eli's great ass flexing in his tight jeans. Oh man, he had to have some of that. Funny, it had been months since he'd had sex. His being gay wasn't something he advertised. When they were on the road, Cal generally abstained unless he felt he could really get away from the press. Fortunately he was a rookie, so they didn't dig too deep -- yet. He didn't want to embarrass the team and make them have to stand up for him. It was easier to just use his hand. Plus he'd been so damned distracted trying to figure out what he wanted to do with his fucking life, he didn't have the energy to pursue and conquer. He knew that fucking contract would be looming. He had to make some decisions fast.

But not tonight, baby. Tonight he was getting the prettiest ass this side of Hollywood. Well, actually this side of Connecticut, since that's where Roan lived with his brother and Em. But Eli gave the model a run for his money. Not as fashion-magazine perfect, but just as beautiful in a quirkier way. Cal practically ran to his car.

Chapter Two

Cal pulled up to the Flamingo parking lot exit, glanced into his mirror, and saw the motorcycle fall in behind him. Fuck. That red rocket between those slim legs was a real turn-on. Not that he needed any more turning on. He pulled into the sparse Long Island traffic, hearing the *vroom* from the bike, and it vibrated straight to his balls as if he was the one with the motorcycle between his legs. Or the rider of the motorcycle. Crap. How fast could he get to the motel?

A couple more minutes down the highway, a very welcome sign said CAVALIER MOTEL. He pulled into the parking lot. As he put the SUV into a space, Eli pulled up beside him. Cal took a deep breath, pulling the mirror down for a second to pretend he was primping. A stall. Why? Was he nervous? Yeah. He didn't do anonymous sex, even when he had the opportunity. He was more a relationship guy, but Eli had pretty much said that was impossible. Could he be happy with just sex? Right now he burned so hot he didn't have a choice.

He popped up the mirror and climbed out. *Jesus!* In one move, the pretty boy had hopped off his bike, grabbed Cal's head, and hauled his lips down for a searching kiss. Sheee-it, this guy meant business of the very best kind. Cal opened his mouth.

Sweet heat. Eli's tongue was soft and wet and hot, exploring the recesses of Cal's mouth. All Cal had to do was hold on and go along for the ride. This guy was no amateur kisser. Qualms or not, he loved this.

Way too soon, Eli pulled back and just stared into Cal's eyes. Cal knew he was shaking but didn't think he could hide it. Didn't really want to.

Eli ran a hand over his arm. "Nervous or excited?"

"Some of both, I think."

"Good." Those full lips curved, and he nodded his head toward the motel lobby. "Want me to get the room?"

Cal took a deep breath. "No, let me. They kind of know me and won't think anything about lack of luggage."

"I'm sure they don't care as long as somebody pays."

"Yeah, well, let me."

Eli grabbed his head, planted a scorching, openmouthed kiss, and then pulled back. "Hurry."

Cal ran for the motel lobby. As he opened the door, he glanced down. Shoot. He pulled his coat closed over his hard-on. The owner remembered him and wanted to chat about soccer. Cal didn't want to be rude. The guy was so nice. Cal answered a few questions and then hurried back to the parking lot. Eli leaned against his bike, long legs stretched out, those amazing curls falling in front of his face. Man, what a picture. As Cal approached, the pretty boy looked up and smiled. Wow. Cal stopped short and stared.

"C'mon, I'm dying here."

Cal covered the space between them in a few long strides, grabbed the smaller man, and pulled him off his feet. Yeah. He got just the reaction he wanted. Eli wrapped those lean thighs around Cal's hungry body. He reached between them and moved his coat aside. *Dream-come-true time.* Eli's hard rod pressed tight against his. Oh God, oh God. Eli wrapped his arms tight around Cal's neck and pumped his body so their erections rubbed like fire sticks. Heat seared through Cal. Coming in his jeans like a teenager would be damned embarrassing. "Jesus."

"Walk, or I'm going to fuck you here."

What? Who *was fucking*? Hell, who cared as long as it was somebody. He could barely breathe, much less walk. Holding his precious burden tight, he half humped, half stumbled to the designated room on the lower floor. As he tried to maneuver the key card from his pocket, Eli leaned in and licked his neck. Holy crap. He fell against the wall. Had to stay on his feet somehow. With one hand, he pushed open the door and lurched inside, flipping on the light.

Just your regular motel room. Bright orange and brown bedspread on a queen-size bed. That was the part Cal cared about. He kicked the door closed, pulled the curtains shut with one hand, and struggled with his beautiful burden to the bed, where he dumped Eli on his back. Jesus, what a sight. Black leather jacket and baby-doll curls. Cal crashed straight down on top of him. God, it was great fucking men. The guy was smaller than Cal but strong as hell. Cal knew his 210 pounds wouldn't crush him. He closed his mouth over those pouty pink lips.

Eli's tongue instantly pressed into Cal's mouth, caressing his tongue top and bottom. He kissed like he wanted to suck Cal's soul through his mouth. The guy's busy hands pulled at Cal's big peacoat and shoved it off his shoulders. Still kissing, Cal completed the job. Crap, he had to get Eli's clothes off. He pulled at Eli's jacket, but some law of physics was clearly fighting him. Two-ten on top did not an easy exit make. Eli pulled back from the kiss. "Not much chance of getting my clothes off this way. What say we both strip and watch? Sound good?"

Sounded perfect. Cal sat up on the edge of the bed and toed off his shoes. Eli sprang up to standing. Cal started to pull off his shirt and froze. Wow. Eli's jacket was off, and now he was pulling the blue T-shirt over his head. Inch by inch, a lean, hard chest as smooth as a baby's butt came into view. Cal's mouth watered. He wanted to lick him all over.

As the curly head emerged, Eli cocked his head. "Your turn."

Cal just stared. The guy was beautiful, but there was something else. Like he had more life in him than other people.

"C'mon, baby. Let me see."

Had to get his clothes off. He pulled his long-sleeved sweater over his head, hurrying so he didn't have to stop looking at Eli for more than a second.

Eli's lips pursed in a silent *ooooh*. Shit, Cal would kill for that reaction. "You next."

Eli leaned over and started pulling off his motorcycle boots. The contrast between the tough boots and the girlie man made Cal smile. He whispered through a dry mouth, "I want more."

Eli kicked the second boot off and looked up. "Do you?" He put his hands on his belt. "Want some of this?"

"Oh yeah."

Eli stood up beside the bed. With agonizing slowness, the man unfastened the belt and began to unbutton the fly of his jeans. *OMG, no fabric underneath. Commando. Jeeeezus.* Soft, curling, golden hair showed behind the fly as he began to lower the jeans. Whoa. He was torn. He didn't want to miss an inch of that beautifully taut body, but his eyes were riveted to the gap in the denim. At last, the prize. A long pink cock, thicker than Cal would have guessed on the slender man, popped from the jeans and slapped against the hard belly. He moaned. Mouthwatering. Nothing girlie about the dick.

"You like?"

"Shit, yes."

"Let me see what I get."

Still staring at that gem of a cock, Cal stood, unfastened his jeans, and pulled, dragging his boxer briefs down at the same time. Not as burlesque as Eli had been, but he got the job done. He knew his cock could be intimidating but figured Eli was not going to run.

A soft laugh made him look from Eli's cock to his face. The man gazed at Cal's crotch. "Well, that's certainly more than a mouthful. Good thing I have a really long tongue." He stuck it out for a second, then began to walk toward Cal, penis bobbing. "Let's put it to work, shall we?"

Eli pushed hard on Cal's shoulders. Cal couldn't catch himself and tumbled onto his back, legs splayed. Eli knelt between Cal's legs and magically produced a condom pack he must have taken out of his jeans.

"Since we don't know each other, I think latex is the order of the day."

Cal nodded, and Eli rolled on the ultrathin. Cal stared as those calloused hands grabbed his cock. Eli lowered his head, then looked up like he wanted to be sure Cal was watching. Hell, yeah. How could he look away? The anticipation alone could give him a heart attack. Slowly, still staring with those golden eyes, Eli applied that wet, soft tongue to the head of Cal's dripping dick. Sweet God. The mushroom head vanished behind soft, bowed lips, and Cal knew where heaven was. Wet, hot, and… Crap! Suction. Hard, deep suction. Mind-altering sucking that pulled his dick far down into the guy's tight throat. And Eli swallowed. Sheee-it!

Too good. Been so long. He didn't want to come too fast. His cock had another idea. Cal couldn't stop his hips from bucking, forcing his rod farther in. "Don't make me come too fast, please."

Eli leaned back. "Baby, this cock doesn't care what your brain wants."

"But I want to fuck you."

The dimpled smile. "You got it all wrong." He slowly licked a drop of precum. "I'm going to fuck you."

Cal got a little chill -- followed by a flash of searing heat. It had been years since he'd bottomed. His size alone generally attracted more submissive men. Who'd have thought Shirley Temple had that kind of balls? And who'd have thought the idea would turn Cal on like a big-screen TV? That cock in his ass? Bring it on! "I'm up for whatever you got."

"Good. I wouldn't want to get rough." Eli flashed a mischievous grin, and Cal burst out laughing. The laughing stopped as Eli deep throated most of Cal's big dick again, then swallowed once, twice. Holy fucking ecstasy. Fire streamed up Cal's spine and ripped into his balls. *No. No. Oh YES.* Flash. Cum shot out of his cock into the condom and the hot, waiting mouth. His body bucked and shook. It didn't end. He never wanted it to end. *Too good to end.*

Still trembling, Cal felt Eli pop his mouth off the still-hard dick and pull off the condom. Then he pushed Cal's legs up. Jesus, cold, slippery wetness surrounded his hole. His aching hole. He wanted this so bad. Who would have thought? Hell, who could think anyway?

A slick finger pushed inside. It had been years. Who cared? Cal practically giggled, he was so relaxed. His ass melted around that wiggling digit. *Oh yeah, two fingers.* In and out. *Mmm, baby.* The fingers came out. "More, please."

"Got my big dominant guy begging?"

"Just do it."

Eli pushed his legs higher. Yeah, maybe later he'd decide to be embarrassed by this pose, but not now. *Just get it in!* A hard, thick rod pushed against the hole, wet and cool. He took a deep breath. This was it. A bottom. His bottom, in fact.

The cock pushed in. Burn, ache, shit, pleasure! He looked over his legs into heavy-lidded gold eyes. Cal wrapped his legs around the slim middle and pulled. The half-mast eyes closed, and a deep moan came out of those soft lips.

Who was on top now? "You like it?"

In answer, Eli began to pump. *Jesus, straight to the prostate.* Cal nearly flew off the bed. He'd forgotten how good that felt. It was great. Sooo great. He'd bottom forever if he could have Eli in his ass.

The blond curls bounced wildly as Eli thrust harder and harder. Gorgeous. A fucking masterpiece. Cal's cock throbbed, ready to explode. Eli was moaning, almost wailing, head thrown back and hips pistoning. *Sheee-it.* Cal exploded cum all over his own chest, splashing on Eli.

The blond yelled, "Oh my God!" as his upper body stiffened, but his hips kept pushing in and out as if they didn't want to stop, ever.

Yeah, Cal knew the feeling.

Finally Eli collapsed onto Cal's sticky chest, making soft mewling noises. Cal's little cat. His jungle cat. He wrapped his arms around Eli. Beautiful Eli. Sometime soon his heart rate would have to approach a non-cardiac-ward level. After a couple of breaths, he rolled Eli to the side and slipped out from under him. He got up and fetched a warm cloth from the tiny bathroom, wiped off his sticky chest, and then rinsed the cloth and returned to the bed.

Eli hadn't moved. Cal didn't think he was asleep, just catatonic. He lay down beside his naked body and gently wiped at the cum drying on the lean chest. Cal found Eli's ear among the sweaty curls. "That was amazing."

The curls bobbed in agreement.

Cal tossed the cooling washcloth toward the bathroom, pulled the bedspread out from under Eli, and got the man settled under the covers. He crawled in, flipped off the light, and wrapped himself around his unmoving body. This was what he wanted more of in his life. More sex and, most of all, this feeling of connection. "You're something pretty special, know that?"

That got Eli's head to turn. In the dim light, the gold eyes shone up at him. Eli said nothing for seconds. Finally: "Yeah, so are you." His head dropped.

Hell, not a completely ringing endorsement. But maybe it was a lot from the guy who said relationship rhymed with commitment. Oh well. After a minute or so of silence, Cal let the comfort of perfect sex drag him under.

* * * * *

Ouch.

Cal opened his eyes to bright light shining around inadequate curtains. Where was he again? Oh yeah, in a motel, lying on his bad shoulder. He flipped onto his back and let his arm stretch. Broken twice, the shoulder's scar tissue was strong but sensitive. He reached his arm out to the side. Cold. Nothing. He turned his head. Nobody.

He knew Eli had been here a little while ago. He had the drained cock to prove it. He'd wakened in darkness and ecstasy, with the other man's lips wrapped around his dick. Who'd have thought he could come that many times in one night? Of course, at twenty-two, he probably wasn't too far gone from the sexual peak they talked about.

He listened for the sound of water. Was Eli in the bathroom?

He sat up and swung his legs over the edge of the bed. Ooookay, the ass hurt a bit. He grinned. But so worth it. In fact, with just a little rest, maybe a shower, he'd be ready to go again. He stood up and laughed. He'd forgotten he had some of these places. He stretched and walked to the closed bathroom door.

"Eli?" He knocked. Quiet. Opening the door, he expected to see the man on the toilet or doing whatever he did to that amazing hair. Empty. Cal turned back into the bedroom. Maybe Eli had left a note saying he'd gone to get coffee or breakfast. He knew better, really. He walked slowly to the window, pushed the curtains aside, and looked out into the parking lot. That would be the lot that had no red motorcycle parked in it.

Dropping the edge of the curtain, he crossed over and sat on the bed. The bed that smelled of cum and some crisp, citrus smell that would forever mean Eli. So he could stay here and convince himself that Eli would be right back -- immediately after pigs became aeronautic. Or he could admit it had been a one-night stand and get over it. What the hell had he expected? Eli's cynical words about lover rhyming with commitment came back to mind.

Hell, all he'd wanted was breakfast.

He headed for the shower. Okay, that wasn't true. Last night had been mind-blowing, and while he hadn't been painting white picket fences, he'd probably had a few more rounds in the sack in mind. Clearly, Eli hadn't shared his vision.

Stepping under the hot water, Cal shrugged and reached for the soap. He didn't even know the guy's last name. He scrubbed his armpits. Maybe he didn't really know his first name either. Well, so that's what one-night stands were about. He'd get over it. He had bigger fish to fry. Was he going to sign the fucking contract? Live his life as an entertainer of screaming fans? A closeted athlete? He had to decide, and fast. He didn't have time to worry about some angel-faced drifter. He didn't have time to wish he could have something that special in his life every day.

Shit. That was such a lie.

24

Chapter Three

Cal pulled into the circular drive and parked next to Roan's Lexus hybrid. The trunk of the black car stood open, suitcases carefully packed inside for their trip to Maine. Cal stared up into the rearview mirror. Maybe this was just what he needed to forget golden eyes and a fucking empty bed. He looked at the beautiful, ultramodern house sprawled on the hillside, surrounded by the brilliance of fall trees. Not a hardship as house-sitting assignments went, even if he did have to play guesthouse contractor supervisor.

He climbed out of the SUV. Em walked -- no, he had to say it -- waddled out the front door, her pregnant belly leading the way. "Hi, darling."

Cal hurried up the front steps. He didn't want her coming down until she had to. He wrapped her in a careful hug. "Hi, sis-in-law."

She laughed. He loved that the great genetic scientist, Dr. Emmaline Silvay, was a member of his family. Well, kind of. The three treated one another as married, so that's how everyone else treated them. He kissed her cheek. "You ready to go?"

"Almost. Roan is carefully listing every doctor, hospital, clinic, chiropractor, and, I think, veterinarian between here and Portland, Maine, in case we need them."

"You up for this trip?"

"Totally. I really want one last quiet time with my guys before we have a new family member. No impossible hours at the company for me and Jake, no multiday photo shoots for Roan. Just the three of us together."

He grinned. "Sounds great. And I get some quiet time too. Works perfectly."

He put his arm around her, and they walked into the house. The beautiful little fountain stream ran through the middle of the entry hall, making a soft rippling sound. In the great room beyond, the soaring wall of glass framed the last of the reds and golds on the trees. It was pretty cool to have a brother-in-law who was both rich and famous. Of course, he also happened to be the sweetest guy on the planet.

Jake bounded down the stairs from the second level with a couple of small bags in his hands. "Hi, baby brother."

Cal embraced him so he didn't have to put the bags down. Jake was tall, but Cal still saw the top of his shaggy golden head. "Hi. You taking the entire house with you?"

"Half."

"You guys making the whole trip in one day?"

"No. Roan found a cool B&B somewhere around halfway. We'll stay there tonight."

Cal cocked his head. "How do the innkeepers react to the three of you being together?"

Em smiled. "We usually book two rooms just for appearances. We use one room for Roan's clothes."

Cal laughed, and Jake headed for the front with his bags. Cal guided Em toward the big sectional sofa. "Might as well sit while the madness continues."

The TV was playing. Cal looked up at a story about some New York financier who was investing a bunch of money in the Rocket Dogs soccer team.

"That's your team, isn't it, Cal?"

He glanced at Em. "Yeah."

"Sounds like this guy is making a serious commitment. This team could be a big deal for you."

"It could." He looked down at his hands.

"But maybe a big deal isn't what you want?"

He grabbed a pillow from the end of the dark gray sectional and put it behind Em's back, keeping the baby belly settled on her lap.

"Hell. I feel like such a whiner. Most people would kill to have a decision like mine to make. Oh poor me. I can sign a contract and probably make millions and contribute that money to all the charities of the world and make a difference in people's lives."

"And the problem is?"

He sighed. "I have to spend my life diving for a ball to do it."

"I thought you loved soccer."

"I do enjoy it. A lot. I just can't get over feeling I'm supposed to do something else with my life. Something…I don't know…more authentic." He glanced at her. "Sorry, that probably sounded really pompous."

"Nope. You need to live your life as you want to."

"Yeah, and if I keep playing, I get to pretend I'm Mr. Macho every day."

"Your team knows you're gay."

"A few people do. The owner, the coach, my roommates. We don't advertise the fact, because football is popular in a lot of places in the world where being gay isn't very well accepted."

"I think that would include here."

"I think it would too."

"Well, at least you can forget all about the team for a few days and relax."

"Yes, that and I can just focus on what I really want without the coach's and owner's ideas getting screamed in my ear."

She patted his hand. "This is really great for us too, dear. We wouldn't mind leaving the house empty, but someone really needs to check in with the contractors occasionally."

"You kidding? This will be a real vacation for me. And it comes right before my decision point. I've got a long-term contract to sign in a few weeks."

"Just remember, what most people want doesn't matter shit. It's your life."

God, he loved her. If he had a woman like her around, he might give bisexuality a try. "Thanks, Em. Mostly I'm just looking forward to being an uncle."

She grinned. He'd hit on her favorite subject. "Yep, this little guy or girl is going to be so spoiled, between the Martin family and my mom. She'll probably head out from California in a VW bus or something."

"Oh c'mon, even Shakti must have graduated to airplanes by now."

"Umm. Maybe. But all that radiation and recycled air..."

Cal laughed. He'd never met Em's hippie mom, but she was a legend throughout the Martin clan. "Seriously, is she coming out after the baby's born?"

"Don't think I could keep her away."

"And you're really not going to find out if it's a boy or girl so we uncles can buy the right presents? You, a master of genetics, can't run one little test?"

Roan's voice rang out from the dining room. "No, we don't want to know. Don't tempt her."

Cal looked up and got the jolt that came from the sight of his brother-in-law. The "most beautiful man in the world," magazines called him, all six feet one of black-haired, green-eyed model perfection. Even though he was so taken, Cal couldn't help a little sigh. Jesus, why did that make him think of Elijah? That was a useless train of thought.

Cal bounded up. "Can I help with anything?"

"Let me take you outside and introduce you to Bill, the contractor. He's great, and really good at his job, so you won't have to do much. Just check in with him and his subs occasionally to answer questions. If you get stuck, you can call me, and I'll arbitrate."

"Great. Lead the way."

A half hour later, Cal had met the contractor and the drywall guys who were working on the guesthouse behind the beautiful main house. It was going to be a plush place. He and Roan walked across the lawn to the French doors leading into the great room. "You sure you want to build this? Nobody's ever going to want to leave."

The model's green eyes sparkled. "Hell, nobody wants to leave now, and they're staying on the same floor as the three of us, which cuts seriously into our sex life. It'll be good to get guests into their own place."

Cal grinned. He didn't want to say that Jake had mentioned Roan really liked to talk dirty during sex and could get pretty loud. Probably TMI for visitors.

They walked in to see Em carrying snacks from the kitchen toward the car, and Jake hauling Cal's duffel up the stairs. He'd be staying in the largest guest room, at the end of the hall, with a view over all the lush fields and gardens that surrounded the house.

Cal closed the French doors behind him and looked again at Roan. "Bill seems like a good guy."

"Yeah, he's on top of things. They'll be changing over from drywall to some of the finish carpentry in a few days. Just check in with those guys and make sure everything's going smoothly. I like to stay kind of close to them whenever new subs come on."

"Will do."

"Looks like Jake got your stuff."

"I think he's trying to move us along."

"Yeah. So you know our cells and where we'll be staying. Call if you need anything."

"I'll try not to do that. You guys need a vacation before the arrival of the vacation killer."

Roan got a soft smile. "I really won't mind giving up a lot of trips for her...or him."

"Hoping for a girl?"

He shook his head. "No, I'll be happy with any configuration."

"But you wouldn't mind having a little model for Dolce, right?"

"Hell, chances are she'll turn out like Em and favor lab coats and jeans."

Jake's voice interrupted. "C'mon, you two. We're packed and ready."

They crossed the great room and entry to the front door. Out in the driveway, Em was already in the shotgun seat, a special extender on her seat belt. Roan hugged Cal and climbed in the back. Jake waved from the driver's side. "Thanks, runt. Eat all the food and watch all the porn you want. Get some rest. Love you."

"Love you back." He waved until they had disappeared down the long, tree-lined drive.

Wow, quiet. Except for the splash of the center fountain and the faint sound of hammers from the back of the property, it was the most silent moment he'd had in months. In the city, he lived with two other soccer players. There wasn't much point in getting an expensive apartment for himself in New York when he was on the road so much of the time. That also put a damper on his sex life.

His roommates were straight, and though they knew he wasn't, he didn't like to make them uncomfortable by bringing home random men. He wasn't really inclined to be promiscuous anyway. If he'd had a boyfriend, it would have been different, but he hadn't had a steady guy since college, more than a year ago. He missed Charlie. No, actually, he missed the idea of Charlie. Having someone special in his life. He thought of the deep caring between Em, Jake, and Roan and sighed. Regular sex wasn't bad either. Of course, he'd never had sex like last night. *Okay, not going there.*

He walked into the house. Even more quiet. No escaping some serious introspection in this house. He sat on the couch, turned the TV back on, and switched to the sports channel, looking for the Rocket Dogs story. After a couple of minutes, an interview with the financier investor came on. Cal got a chill. Man, the billionaire was one cool and charming guy. He spoke with great enthusiasm about the future of the team and bringing together all the best talent. Shit. One more force to be reckoned with.

Cal cocked his head. He was familiar. Like déjà vu or something. Had Cal met him before? No, he would remember. But there was something about the guy… He shook his head and switched off the TV. He didn't have to dive headfirst into the middle of the decision, did he? Maybe he'd go to the media room and watch *Funny Girl*. At least here, he could be gay.

Chapter Four

He needed a good fuck.

Cal stretched his mostly bare body as he enjoyed the November sun filtering through glass and climate-controlled air in the sunroom. It certainly hadn't taken him long to get used to the lap of luxury. He'd been a good boy for two days, checking carefully on the guesthouse progress. Things were under control there without him. He'd packed in nine or more hours of sleep a night and some serious hot-tub time, so he was starting to feel like regular humans who didn't throw their bodies through the air trying to catch random soccer balls. He'd also done some serious eating.

What was next? Sex. *Okay, small Eli twinge.* Maybe there was a gay bar around here somewhere. While he wasn't much for one-night stands, it could be nice to find a man to hang out with for a few days or a week. He should have asked the guys, but in truth, they probably wouldn't know. They'd been a couple when they moved into this house they'd built, and Em had come along less than a year later. No need for prowling. Man, he'd like that too. Staying home for what he needed. He sure wasn't embarked on a life that encouraged staying at home much ever. But that was a thought for some other time. Maybe he'd look online later to find a bar.

He grabbed his towel and dried the sweat pooling in his Speedos. Wouldn't be caught dead in these things in public, but they were great for sunning. Hauling himself up, he headed for the kitchen. Lunch was in order. They'd left him a refrigerator and pantry full of goodies. Roan the Gourmet had probably orchestrated it, but Jake had thrown in his share of junk food.

As he passed the entry, the doorbell rang. Who the hell? Maybe someone connected with the construction. He couldn't run upstairs and change, so he wrapped his towel around his hips to cover the practically nonexistent bathing suit. Yeah, he'd bought it in France.

Cal pulled open the door and was surprised to see a really cute young guy. Small, maybe five feet eight or so, and quite slim, with dark brown hair that kind of curved around his ears. He was wearing fatigue pants and a leather jacket and, WTF, had a duffel bag over his shoulder. What was he selling? "Can I help you?"

The guy's eyes were wide, and he seemed pretty riveted on Cal's bare chest. Good, the kid was intimidated. "I, uh… Is, uh, Emmaline Silvay here?"

"No, she's on vacation. I'm her brother-in-law. What can I do for you?" Cal was conscious of stretching out his six-five for effect.

The kid dropped the duffel on the wide portico floor. "Merde. I knew I should've called, but I got this great flight, and my cell was freaking out from being back in the States, and I couldn't get a connection, so I just came." He looked up. "Vacation, really?"

"Yeah, really."

"But she shouldn't be flying."

"Actually, she's not. She's driving, if that's any of your business."

"Well, it kind of is. I'm Em's cousin, Angel Silvay. She asked me to come help deliver her baby."

"What?" Was this guy a doctor? Angel? He didn't look Hispanic.

"Yeah, I've been on a mission in Senegal. Still am, actually. I mean, I've got to go back. But I got a cargo flight to bring me to New York, and then I got a bus out here."

Cal looked at his bag. "So you're planning on staying? Here?"

"Well, yeah. I don't have any other place to stay and not much money. Em said I could stay here."

"Why the hell didn't she tell me?"

The kid looked down at his sneakers. "I'm earlier than expected. I saw the chance for the flight and jumped at it. I guess I can go into the city and try the Y."

Oh shit, who was he to put Em's cousin out on the street, even if it did wreck his plans for some hot sex in the Jacuzzi? Besides, the guy was really cute. Big brown eyes. Probably about Cal's age. Guess it was too much to hope he was gay. "Come on in, then." Cal stepped aside, allowing access into the entry hall.

"You sure?"

"No."

The kid stopped walking.

"Sorry, I'm being an ass. It's just that this is my vacation too, and I wasn't planning on sharing the space with anyone. Come on in."

The kid walked into the house. "*Mon dieu*, it doesn't look like we're going to be crowded."

"No. What's with the French?"

The kid still stared around the house. "It's the colonial language of Senegal. It's the one language most of the people all know, so I have to know it too. I just get used to speaking it."

"Ah." Cal nodded.

The guy grinned. "I'm probably wrecking your plans for hot and cold running cheerleaders."

"Only if the cheerleaders are guys."

The boy stared at Cal's chest, then slowly up to his face. "Really?"

"Yes, really. If that bothers you…"

"Hell no. It's just you're such a hunk." He smiled. "Never assume, right?"

Cal smiled back. "Guess you're not gay, or you wouldn't assume that only women deserved hunky guys."

He shook his head. "No, not gay. And I guess I just didn't think about it. But gotta admit, some guy's pretty lucky."

Odd thing for a straight guy to say. "Uh, thanks. C'mon, let me show you your room."

He led Angel upstairs and installed him in the guest room farthest from where Cal was staying. It had a soft, gray-blue decor, a king-size bed like all the guest rooms but one, and a balcony that looked out over the front of the house. "After you clean up, there's a ton of food around this place. I'm not much of a cook, but help yourself."

"Oh, I love to cook. Never get much chance in Senegal, 'cause all we've got most of the time is wood fires. Okay if I cook something?"

"You kidding? Hell, yes. Wait till you see Roan's gourmet kitchen."

"Roan. He's the mannequin, uh, model, right?"

Good, he must already know about his cousin's living arrangements. "Yeah, and a nicer guy you'll never meet. My brother's pretty great too."

"That's Jake, right? The scientist."

"Yep. Geneticist. He and Em work together."

"Oh dieu, I sure heard all about him for a year or so."

"Yeah, seems they had the hots for each other, but neither one would step up and say so. They finally got together." He pointed to the bathroom. "All the bathrooms in this house are pretty great, so get comfortable. I'm going to shower the sweat off me. By the way, I was in the sunroom. I don't usually flash the callers."

"You don't hear me complaining, *bebe*."

Cal seriously wanted to ask the guy again if he was gay, but figured he better take Angel's word. "Okay, make yourself at home. I'm no host, so you're on your own."

"Fine by me. See you later maybe."

"If you're cooking, I'm eating."

The kid laughed, and Cal headed for his suite.

He passed the linen closet. Towels. Probably none in the guest room except some decorative shit. He opened the closet and grabbed four of the thick, soft bath sheets he loved so much. Hell, Angel probably hadn't seen a fluffy towel in Africa. He deserved a little luxury.

He knocked lightly on the half-open guest room door. No answer. He pushed the door and heard water running. He thought he'd better take them in, so Angel would see them when he got out. He crossed the room on the soft Asian rugs and opened the bathroom door. "Hey, Angel, here are… Holy *shit*!"

Standing naked and dripping inside the open shower door was a tall, very slim girl. Almost flat-chested, but not completely, her combination of perky little breasts and curling pubic hair made her sex pretty damned clear. Now.

She just stared back at him. "Did you expect me to be clothed in the shower, *mon ami*?"

"No, I… Jesus, why didn't you tell me? I mean…"

She reached out and took one of the towels he still clutched in his hands and began to dry herself with it. "Why didn't I tell you what?"

"That you're a fucking girl?"

She stopped drying and stared at him. Recovering, she frowned. "Well, what in the hell else would I be?"

He backed out of the steamy room. "Sorry. I'm really sorry."

He made it out the door, turned, and headed back to his suite. Jesus, he was sharing the house with a girl. A damned cute girl, uh, boy. Whatever. What exactly did he think about that?

He got in the shower, took his time washing, then turned on the TV and watched a game show. *Okay, Martin, face the music. You can't avoid her forever.* He dressed in jeans and a T-shirt and opened his bedroom door. Yum. Appetizing smells drifted up the stairs. Maybe seeing her naked hadn't been a deal breaker on dinner.

He padded down the stairs barefoot and across the great room to the big island that separated the kitchen from the larger space. She was at the oven, back turned, dancing a little to the music coming from the sound system. Obviously she'd figured out how to work it.

Even knowing she was a girl, it was mind-boggling how boyish she looked. Long, coltish legs, slim hips in slightly baggy jeans, strong, tanned arms coming from a short-sleeved linen shirt she could easily have bought in the young boys' department. The short, shaggy brown hair brushed her collar.

Cal watched her cute butt move to the music. Whoa. Getting a little cock reaction there. He'd been with women. Didn't mind fucking them, but wasn't usually attracted to them. It was hard to explain. "Hi."

She turned. Would she smile or was she still mad? She grinned. "Hi, oh not-too-observant one."

He hung his head. "I said I'm sorry."

"Actually I'm teasing you. It happens a lot, and I even encourage it."

"Why?"

"Women aren't always treated that well in parts of Africa. There's things they can't do, places they can't go. Being thought a boy can be helpful."

"So I'm not a complete loser?"

"Don't know about that part, *mon grand*." She grinned again. "But a lot of people think I'm a guy."

"If it makes you feel any better, you're a damned cute guy."

She swept a deep bow. "*Merci*, mon ami."

He felt the heat of the blush and quickly pointed to the piles of food on the countertops. "What can I do to help?"

"Sit there and talk to me. I get a kick out of this."

He settled onto a high, upholstered stool. "What are you making?"

"Chicken cordon bleu."

"You're kidding?"

She looked up from the stove. "Don't you like it?"

"Are you serious? I'm in heaven. You and Roan must be blood brothers...uh, kin. Whatever."

"I figured somebody was a serious chef. Look at this layout." She gestured to the professional, six-burner stove, the prep sink, the wine cooler. Yeah, Cal guessed it was pretty impressive.

"He wants to retire from modeling and take up cooking."

"Well I've seen his picture, so that would be modeling's loss."

"Ain't that the truth."

He did help put the salad together. Angel showed him how to tear the lettuce so as not to "bruise it with a knife." She'd set places at the dining room table, and he was feeling pretty fancy, leaning back in the comfy pumpkin-colored chairs, drinking some of Roan's favorite wine. Beaujolais, she'd said. Whatever, it was damn good. And the food? "This is seriously delicious."

"Thanks. A lot of the time in Senegal, I'm squatting in front of an open fire with a chicken somebody killed for me that afternoon."

"I didn't realize."

"It's a country of great contrasts. Some very rich and privileged, and a lot of poor. Or what we'd call poor. Poverty is a little different when it's a shared way of life rather than a subculture."

"So you're a doctor?"

She looked at him sharply. "No, why'd you think that?"

"You said you were going to deliver Em's baby."

"Yes, and I'm eminently qualified to do it. I'm a midwife."

He sipped his wine appreciatively. "I thought that was kind of a historical thing."

She frowned a little. "It is. It's an ancient profession. Since before recorded history. But in the US it really came on in the 1920s, when people couldn't afford to go to doctors."

"Why would they use one today? I mean in Africa, sure. But Em?" The frown got deeper. Okay, that wasn't the most diplomatic question on earth.

"Em is a smart lady. She knows when you birth with a midwife you're more likely to have a relaxed experience without all the medical bullshit. Midwives reduce the number of C-sections and episiotomies."

He didn't know what that last thing was, but whatever. "Em's almost forty. Doesn't she need to be in a hospital?"

"She's thirty-eight, hardly old, except to a cute junior like you."

Excuse me?

"If I find she or the baby is having any distress, we'll have her doc standing by. Otherwise it should be easy-peasy. She's strong and healthy. Her body knows what to do, and so do I."

"What do you mean 'junior'? We're probably the same age."

She smiled like a cute little cat. "And how old is that?"

"I'm twenty-two."

"I'm twenty-nine, junior, and I've delivered hundreds of babies. Any more questions?"

He crossed his arms and resisted saying *harrumph*. "Well, you don't look it."

"Thanks."

He was interested in her job, though. "So how do you get to work in Africa?"

"I'm with a worldwide charity called Global Outreach. We provide services to third-world countries, including a lot of health care and social services."

Social services? "I have a degree in sociology."

"No kidding? Social workers are sorely needed in Africa. So many people require help and can't get it. Actually, gay men are one of the most oppressed groups. You can be killed in Africa for being gay."

"Hell, you can get killed here for being gay."

"Yes, but here it's the exception, not the rule, and it's not condoned. In Africa a gay man has few rights. It's almost impossible for them to get health care even when they're dying. It's sad." She sipped her wine. "So what do you do? Are you a social worker?"

"Uh, I'm a goalie for a professional soccer team, the Rocket Dogs." For one second, he felt wounded. Most people thought being a pro soccer player was cool. *Jeez, suck it up.* She was just reflecting his own feelings. Being a pro athlete was great for lots of people, but clearly this woman thought being a social worker was cooler. And what the hell, maybe he did too. He shrugged. "Yeah, well, sometimes physiology is destiny, you know."

She cocked her head. "If you choose it to be." She started clearing a few plates from the table, and he hopped up to help. She brought in some fresh fruit and cheese, and they sat again to enjoy it.

He poured them both a little dessert wine she'd found in the wine refrigerator in the kitchen. Yum. Just a tiny bit sweet, cool and crisp. Roan knew how to live.

She sipped and closed her eyes. "This is such luxury after where I've been." She opened her big brown eyes, and they sparkled as she smiled. "So what have you got planned for fun?"

"Nothing planned except a TV movie and bed."

"What about the cheerleaders? The *boy* cheerleaders, that is? There must have been some plans of yours I wrecked by showing up and being a girl."

She really was cute. "I kind of thought of finding a gay bar, but I don't know the area very well. I live in the city."

"Have you gone online?"

"Not yet."

"Hey, I'm great at research. I'll find you a gay bar, no problem."

How did he feel about that? "Okay."

"Tell you what. I'll search some tonight and see if I can find some comments and reviews." Why did this girl look so mischievous? "But if I find a good place, will you take me with you?"

Hell no! He started to protest, but she rushed on.

"See, I love to dance, and it's no fun going to places alone. Plus I don't have a car. And I figure gay guys probably like to dance too, right? So if I find a place with dancing, I could go, and if they thought I was a guy, that wouldn't hurt, since I figure not everybody hooks up at these places, right? If you hook up, well, we'll figure out about the car, okay?" She'd gone from kitten to puppy, practically bouncing in her chair.

"And if some guy, some gay guy, starts grinding against you on the dance floor, and you don't have the necessary equipment, what then?"

She peeked up under her eyelashes. "Socks?"

He burst out laughing. She was damned cute. "You're crazy."

"Well, I could always make a run for it."

Chapter Five

She'd talked him into it.

Walking toward the Blade gay bar, Angel bobbed ahead of him, apparently oblivious to the cold, and bouncing with enthusiasm. He had to admit she looked seriously cute. Actually the word was *hot*, but he wasn't going there.

She'd traded the baggies for a trim pair of skinny jeans. It was a testament to her boyishness that she still didn't look feminine, despite the way the denim hugged her hips. She'd worn a slightly baggy T-shirt, and what breasts she had were squashed under some kind of camisole thing she'd revealed while they were in the kitchen by pulling her T-shirt up to her face. Over it all, she wore a trim leather jacket that was definitely unisex. And it was green, kind of a yellowy green color. Really pretty with her hair and creamy skin, but not too girlie for a fashionable gay guy to pick. She topped -- or maybe bottomed -- off the whole outfit with cool Converse sneakers. A perfect little twink.

What about her voice? Would guys immediately know she wasn't a boy? He hadn't. Lots of young guys had higher voices, and so did lots of gay guys. Like Elijah. He winced and shied from the thought. *Get a grip, Martin. You're supposed to be looking for sex, not worrying about Angel -- or Eli.*

She'd gotten to the entrance first and waited for him. The place was pretty subdued. Just a small sign and a pleasant country-home exterior. Very Connecticut. But he saw what he expected was cigarette smoke coming from a driveway at the side of the club. Probably some outdoor action going on there. She pulled open the door before he could do it. Yeah, had to remember not to treat her like a girl.

Inside? Not so subdued. A live band was playing pop music fronted by a girl with a gravelly, sexy voice. Interesting. There was a bar along the wall, not quite as big as the one at the Flamingo, but a much bigger dance floor. Male couples and a few female pairs filled the floor, hugging tight, but with no overt grinding. Good. For Angel, at least.

A man who looked like he'd be more at home in a political campaign than a gay bar stood behind a small reception podium. He surveyed the two of them and pointed a finger toward Angel. "Is he old enough?"

Oh shit. He hadn't thought about the carding thing.

Angel laughed. "Sure. See." She held out a license. Had she been holding it all along? Fortunately the host glanced but didn't take it. Somewhere on that card, probably under Angel's finger, was an incriminating *F* for female. The host looked Angel up and down. "You're a pretty boy." He nodded at Cal. "This your boyfriend?"

She smiled. "Just a friend."

The preppy guy leaned toward her. "Look me up before you leave."

"Thanks. But I'm just here to dance."

"I like to dance. Maybe when I get off at two?"

Cal grabbed her arm. "C'mon, Angel."

She looked back at the host as Cal dragged her away. "Thanks. That's past my bedtime."

He gave her arm a little jerk. "What was that all about?"

"Just making friends."

He hauled her toward a small table that was opening up as two men, clearly intent on things that topped Cal's priority list, moved toward the entrance.

Angel wouldn't be hauled. As they passed the dance floor, she just started bobbing and weaving. Cal couldn't hold her, and she slipped onto the floor by herself. In seconds two guys had split their couple and were dancing around her. She threw her head back and laughed, tight butt wriggling.

Cal hurried to grab the table, sat, and looked back. He could just make her out in the middle of the moving crowd.

Okay, time to do some serious scoping. He turned in his chair so he could survey the men at the tables and the bar. A few were alone. A couple of nice-looking men. His come-hither look was a bit rusty. Maybe if he just looked available.

A harried waiter leaned in to the table, and Cal ordered a beer. What did Angel want? Hell, make it two beers.

The beer arrived pretty quickly, although Cal couldn't figure how the waiter moved that fast in the crowd. He took a sip. *How does an available man look? Alone.* Yeah, that's what he was.

He saw an attractive blond over at the bar, looking at him. Hmm. Likely candidate. But the blond hair wasn't curly, and he bet those eyes weren't gold. He glanced again toward the dance floor. That sure was one cute butt.

* * * * *

Oh merde, when was the last time she'd had this much fun? Angel circled the two dancers who were partnering her. Both cute. Thought she was a boy, obviously, because they were flirting like mad. They must not be a couple. But at the moment, it was all about the dancing.

She looked over toward the table. Oh. Yeah, well Caleb had found himself some really attractive company. They were sitting together, heads close, sipping beer. She wanted to be happy for him. She'd try. But this was one gay guy she wished wasn't. First, gorgeous. Way prettier than he realized. Tall and lean, with that wild, brown and blond mixed hair that looked like he spent his life in the sun. And the clear blue eyes that crinkled at the edges when he smiled. Plus, he was nice and smart and fun despite the fact that she'd pretty much wrecked his vacation. Oh well. She did a spin, and one of the men grabbed her hand and circled her just as the song ended.

She fell back a couple of steps. Bam, solid wall. Warm wall. Hands grabbed her shoulders. She looked up into black eyes that shone with naughty intent.

44

The dancer smiled, revealing a row of even, white teeth. *Yeah, the better to eat you with.* "Hi, pretty."

"Hi."

"I'm Carlos. You want to dance with me?" His voice danced with a smooth Latino accent.

The music had changed to slow and sultry. Hmm. Maybe not such a good idea. "Okay."

She slipped into his arms. He was tallish, maybe five-eleven, and the hair was as black as the eyes. Pret-ty. "I'm Angel."

He cocked his head. "Angel?" He pronounced it "Ahn-hel," in the Spanish fashion.

"Yeah, I guess. But it's Americanized." She neglected to mention that it was short for Angelica.

He pulled her in close. *Okay, need to keep a little distance here.* It felt nice to be close to a man, even if he was gay. She'd broken up with Mitchell months ago, and her crazy schedule made a social life -- read sex life -- pretty sparse.

She felt soft lips against her ear. "You really are a pretty one."

"Thanks." She gulped a little. This guy was so sexy. She wasn't used to such overt sensuality.

He pulled her a little tighter, and she could feel his stiff erection pressing on her abdomen. Again, she tried to pull away without being insulting, but she was about to get outed, and not in a good way.

His lips were on her ear again. "Don't worry, Ahn-hel. I know your secret, and it's safe with me."

She pulled back. What the --

He smiled at her with those teeth again. "I know you're a girl, pretty, and I like it just fine."

Trapped. She looked down at her sneakers, then back at him. "Look, I'm sorry. I don't want to make trouble or hurt anybody. I just love to dance, and when my friend was coming here, I tagged along."

"I'm not complaining, pretty. I like pussy as much as I like cock."

He was cute but -- "I don't remember offering either one."

He laughed. "Maybe we'll get to that decision later. Is it because of tall and handsome over there?"

She looked toward Cal, still deep in flirtatious conversation. Sigh. "No, he's just a friend. And he's gay."

"Oh, I don't know, pretty. Looks a bit bi-curious to me, way he was starin' at your ass."

Really? "Nah. He's just looking out for me. My cousin's his sister-in-law."

"Maybe." The music changed to a rumba. "Right now, I want to dance."

Had he requested this music? The rumba was her favorite, and she melted into his arms as the sensuous rhythm surrounded them. Man, he could dance.

It only took a couple of minutes to remember why the rumba was called the dance of love. Hips pressed tight and swaying, legs entwined, it was sex on a dance floor. Maybe she'd rather her partner was taller, with brown-gold hair, but this guy was pretty persuasive. Sloooow. Ummm. Perfect unison. He dipped her low and then pulled her in tight against his chest, lips pressed against her cheek. Jeez. His tongue caressed the side of her mouth. She closed her eyes and went with it. The feeling of a man's arms, the press of his hard thighs -- yikes.

She was pulled backward, not hard but enough to separate her from Carlos and his questing tongue. Strong hands gripped her shoulders. "Excuse me, but I'd like to cut in."

She looked up into those blue, blue eyes.

"Hang on." Carlos started to grab her back, but Cal was hard-bodied and very, very tall. A formidable man. He also didn't look like he was kidding. Obviously recognizing the better part of valor, Carlos gave a sweeping bow. "I never get between a man and the lady he came with." He winked at her. "Hope I see you again sometime, pretty." The handsome Latino walked away into the crowd, hips swaying.

She looked up at Cal. "Do you really want to dance, or just to get me away from Carlos?"

He frowned. "I said I did, didn't I?" He took her in his arms, and after a little fumbling with how to properly grasp her smaller body, he began to move. Hmm. Not Carlos, but not bad.

"What did he mean by 'lady he came with'? Was he just being facetious?"

"No, he knew I was a girl."

Cal's frown got deeper. "He sure as hell didn't seem to mind."

"Nope. Said he liked pussy as much as he liked cock."

Cal stared at the space where Carlos had retreated. "Asshole."

"Good dancer, though."

"Yeah, I noticed. Sort of the coat-of-paint variety, I'd say."

She giggled. He was cute when he was -- what? Mad? Jealous? Not likely. Just big-brother protective. "I appreciate the white knight routine, but I would've been okay. He's harmless."

He held her away from him and looked into her face. "That dude is anything but harmless. And this place has a pretty active alley scene, if you haven't noticed."

Actually she hadn't. "Thanks."

They danced quietly for a couple of minutes. It was hard not to run her hands over all those taut muscles under his shirt. God, what was it about him? She was used to taking care of herself. She'd faced terrorists and violent husbands and fathers pretty much alone. But with Cal, she felt -- protected, safe. Yeah, stupid. What the hell would she want with those things?

She looked up at his face. He was staring off into space. "So why are you here with me? Why don't you dance with that cute guy I saw you with? I'll go sit and be quiet and stay out of trouble. Go on."

He shook his head.

"Why not? You two looked really interested. C'mon, it's a big house. I don't mind if you bring somebody home with us."

"Thanks. But the guy just wasn't my type."

She looked around. "Hey, there're lots of other guys around here."

She felt his body stiffen. "Angel, I'm not interested."

What was with him? "So you want to go?"

He looked almost angry. "Yeah."

She grabbed her jacket from the bar stool she'd thrown it on, and he got his from the table. As she passed the dance floor, Carlos waved. "Adios, pretty. See if I'm not right about the curiosity."

Oh, she bloody well wished.

Chapter Six

Trees lined the roads to the house. So different from New York. Quiet, wooded. He glanced over at Angel, bobbing in her seat to some imagined music. Why the hell was he with this woman instead of some guy from the bar? Why did he think she was so cute? Dancing with her had been, well, sexy, and he'd watched the other men in the club glancing at him like they were wishing they were the ones with the adorable boy. Even the feel of her under his hands hadn't been what he thought of as feminine. Her body was lean and strong, not soft and round. Maybe because he'd originally thought she was a guy, he just couldn't shake the feelings.

"Hey, Cal. Can I ask you something? You don't have to answer."

"Yeah, you're right, I don't have to. Spit it out."

"You said that guy you were talking to in the bar wasn't your type. Can I ask why? What didn't you like about him?"

He grinned. "Why? Are you looking to become my yenta? Want to fix me up with the right man?"

"I don't know. I guess I just want to know more about you."

He wasn't sure how he felt about that, but he also wasn't sure how to answer. Why *wasn't* that guy his type? He could barely remember the man's name, he'd been so distracted by Angel. He'd been good-looking and pleasant. Seemed smart enough and definitely interested. The answer forced its way out of his mouth. "Actually I met someone about a week ago." He sensed Angel looking at him, and he glanced over. She had a funny expression, like maybe she was disappointed or something. He looked back at the road.

"A man you're interested in?"

"Yeah. No. I mean it was a one-night stand." He didn't say he'd hoped for it to be more. "But there was something about him I'm… Shit, I don't know what I'm saying."

"Something you really liked? Something you want to find again?"

"Yeah. I guess so. I just know the guy in the bar didn't have it."

"Why don't you find him again? The one-nighter?"

"I don't even know his name. I mean his last name, or anything else about him."

"Hmmm." She leaned onto the console intently. "So let's figure out what you liked about him, and maybe that will help you find it again."

"Ah, so you really are a matchmaker."

"Yeah, we midwives want everybody to settle down and have babies. Keeps us in work." He caught her grin from the corner of his eye.

"Uh, I think you may be barking up the wrong tree trying to fix me up with a guy then."

"Nope. I figure you find the right guy, get a surrogate, or maybe do a ménage thing like Em and Roan and Jake. That's working out for my career."

He laughed. The way he felt this evening, that wasn't out of the question.

"Okay, so what did you like? About the guy, I mean."

"Funny thing is, he looks sort of like a girl. You know, like you resemble a boy? He's got blond curls and pink cheeks and a curvy mouth. And he's slim, but really hard-bodied, you know, kind of like you."

Her voice was soft in the darkness. "So you like the way he looks? You like androgynous people, uh, men?"

"I never thought about it before. I was with one guy for a long time in college. But, yeah, I guess Charlie was pretty girlie-looking for a boy."

"And have you ever been with women, girls?"

"A few times in high school and college, when I was still trying to figure out if my tendencies were for real."

"I imagine it's no small thing, deciding you're gay in our society."

"Hell, no. You gotta be pretty damned sure before you put all the people you love in that position."

"I'd think you'd worry more about yourself. When did you come out?"

"It was kind of gradual. First my friends, then my folks. I still haven't really come out to the world. I never announce my orientation, for the sake of the team."

"Hell, Caleb, you sure worry about other people a lot."

He glanced at her. "Don't you?"

"Yeah, but I give myself a fair shake too."

Did he think about what other people wanted too much? His family was so heroic in his eyes -- firefighters, nurse, charity executive, scientist -- he wanted so much to make them all proud. Of course, he knew they loved him no matter what, but he still wanted to make a mark among them.

Her voice broke into his thoughts. "So what happened with the girls?"

"What?"

"When you dated the females?"

"I never minded having sex with them. I just was never really attracted to them."

She snorted. "How does that work?"

"I mean, I'd decide to take out a girl because she was the type my friends and fraternity brothers thought was hot. I just couldn't see her that way. But once we got into it, the sucking and fucking was all pretty stimulating. It's just if a girl walks down the street, I'm not likely to pay attention." He didn't add *except for you*.

"So did you like anything else about this guy except his looks and his hard body?"

Cal could feel himself blushing, the family curse. "I didn't exactly have a life-goals discussion with him. I said it was a one-night stand. You know this is kind of an embarrassing conversation to have with a girl."

She laughed that cute chortle. "Don't think of me as a girl. Think of me as a friend. Maybe a guy friend. Make that a gay-guy friend, since straight males never talk about anything personal."

He already thought of her way too much as a guy. "Okay. Well, he had an intensity, a passionate way about him. And even though he was very girlie-looking, he was" -- he could feel the blush again -- "kind of dominant."

"*You* like to be dominated?"

"No. Shit, I --"

"Sorry. I didn't mean that. Of course, all strong men like to give up control sometimes. Really, it makes perfect sense."

"I'm not talking about whips and chains here."

She petted his arm. "Even if you were, it makes sense. I'm sorry I was surprised."

They were driving down the long entryway to the house. He was quiet for a minute. "Anyway, we just sort of connected."

"But you didn't arrange to see him again?"

Quiet. "When I woke up, he was gone."

Another pause. "I'm sorry, Cal. Every woman knows what that's like, at least to some degree."

Yeah, he supposed that was true.

He parked in the space to the side of the circular drive. Enough heavy reflection. "So, have you got my type all nailed down?"

She grinned. "I'm working on it."

* * * * *

People. People who need people… Barbra's silky voice poured through the multichannel sound system surrounding Cal on the couch. What the fuck was up? Why was he lying here thinking about a girl, for crap's sake? He was gay. True, he'd had sex with women, and a lot of the gay guys he knew never had and never wanted to. So he didn't gag over pussy, but all his instincts pointed to guys. Always had. What was it about this girl? He heard Roan's voice in his head. *"Yeah, I'm gay, but sometimes there's this one woman."* Was Angel his "one woman"? And what she'd said about being dominated. What the fuck?

* * * * *

Angel crawled into bed with a book she'd found on the shelves of the great room. It sounded kind of romantic. She'd try it. She pulled the covers up to her shoulders, since she preferred to sleep nude. The house was warm, but she'd cracked the window a little for fresh air. Settling in, she lay on her side with the book propped in front of her.

Romantic. So Cal was in love with a guy with curly hair. Maybe not in love, but clearly in lust. Sigh. She felt bad for him. Waking up alone after a great night of sex was a shock to the system. Chances were he hadn't been rejected by that many lovers. Of course, he was young, so he likely hadn't had that many. She felt a little bad for herself too. She hadn't been attracted to anyone since Mitchell had left. Of course, she hadn't really been attracted to Mitchell at the end there. They'd worn out their welcome together. But Cal was attractive. Really attractive. Damn shame.

She turned to page one and started reading. By page thirty-four, her eyes were swimming a bit, and she figured she'd give it up.

Tap tap. Hmm. No ravens present. It could only be Cal. She pulled the covers up higher. "Come in."

His tall body filled the whole doorway. "Can I ask you something?"

53

"Sure." Holding the cover close, only her bare arms and shoulders showing, she scooted back against the pillow so she was sitting up more. "Shoot."

He sat on the edge of her bed. Perched might be the accurate word, like he might fly at any moment. "Why did you say you knew strong people sometimes like to be dominated?"

Aha. She knew she'd hit a nerve. "I knew a couple when I lived in the commune with Shakti and Em. He was a big dominant alpha guy, and she was a mild-mannered housewife. Except in the bedroom. There, she called the shots. Like you said, not whips and chains, but she 'topped' him, so to speak."

"How do you know that?"

"Observation. Hearing stuff, as kids do. Things were a bit more open in the commune than other places. I didn't completely understand it at the time, but looking back, I think the man wanted someone he trusted to be in charge of him. He didn't have to worry about making her come or satisfying her. She saw to that. She asked for what she wanted, and he gave it. And she looked out for what he wanted. I think it really worked for them. But the commune wasn't exactly your average American community." She smiled. "Or then again, maybe it was."

"Interesting. Are you like that?"

"Like what?"

He shrugged, and she saw that blush she noticed frequently. "Kind of dominant. You know, asking for what you want?"

Whoa. Where did that question come from? "A little bit. I think one of the big problems with my last relationship was he wanted to be in charge, but he didn't really care about anyone but himself. When I tried to get what I needed, he thought I was being pushy and domineering. He hated it."

He looked down at his hands. "Do you find me attractive?"

Double whoa. That was not the question she'd expected. "I think you know I do." She almost made a wisecrack about what a shame it was she had to pine in unrequited lust, but she decided to see where this interesting line of questioning went.

"Would you...?" He took a deep breath. Started again. "Would you ever want to have sex with me?"

She knew her mouth was hanging open. Not a wisecrack in sight. "I would love to have sex with you. May I ask why you want to know?"

He stared into space. Less threatening, she assumed. "Because I don't know why, but I really think you're sexy. I hope you don't mind, but it probably has something to do with your looking like a boy, kind of." He glanced at her, then away. "Do you mind?"

"No. I have no illusions about being some female sex goddess. I know I'm boyish. I even like it. I guess I think it makes me unique."

He looked at her again. "It does." Back at the hands. "See, it's been a long time since I had sex with a woman. I was young and didn't much know or care how to make a woman, uh, satisfied. So I thought if..."

"You thought if I was responsible for that, you wouldn't have to worry?"

"Yes, exactly."

Holy merde! The guy was seriously asking to have sex with her. She tried not to leap at him. She leaned forward, still holding the covers to her chest. "Maybe we should test your interest a little."

He leaned back and frowned. "What do you mean?"

"I look really boyish in clothes. Maybe that's what you're attracted to. Under the clothes, I don't have a ton of female equipment, but it is there. Maybe that will turn you off."

He still looked pretty suspicious. "Maybe. But I have seen women naked, including you briefly. Hardly repulsive."

She'd risen up on her knees. "See what you think in a more sexual context." She dropped the covers.

His eyes widened, and then he cocked his head as if surveying from a better angle. "You really are flat-chested."

Should she slap him or laugh? Laughing won, since it was so the truth.

He reached out and touched the very slight rise of her breast. "I've seen guys with more boobs than this." By now he was laughing too.

She waggled her hips, pointing to her trimmed pussy. "But the question is, have you ever seen a guy with one of these?"

"Turn around."

She did as he asked.

"Jeeeezus. That is the ass I've been staring at all night. That is an award-winning ass, I don't care what sex you are."

She stopped laughing. "Don't you?"

He reached down and pulled his T-shirt over his head.

Oh dieu, there was that beautiful chest, hard and hairless. Still on her knees, she turned her upper body toward him. "Then why don't you take off your pants and show me what you've got to put in this ass, mon grand."

He gaped, then grabbed for the button on his jeans and started unfastening, still staring at her waggling behind.

She watched as the tops of his boxer briefs came into view. *Okay, let's show him who's dominant. "Se presser.* Hurry."

He stuck his fingers in the tops of the briefs, stood up, and in one motion, pulled the jeans and underwear down his legs. Then he stepped out and kicked. She barely saw that part, because she was staring at a really big, wet, dripping cock pulsing against his abdomen. No, he didn't seem to mind her being female one bit. But would she be able to accommodate that monster in her butt? She'd had experience, but not on quite such a grand scale. Oh, she was going to enjoy finding out.

She reached out her hand, and he took it. She pulled, and he knelt on the bed, big cock bobbing.

"That's something special you've got there."

He grinned, though he looked pretty nervous. "Glad you like it."

"I'd like to suck it."

"Be my guest."

She pulled again, and he let himself fall onto the bed, then rolled over with the big rod sticking up. She dived, grabbed, and swallowed. Or at least tried to. He was more than a mouthful. She licked around the ripe head and then more slowly took it in inch by inch. He moaned and pushed upward. *Whoa.* She backed off a little to keep from getting choked. *Okay, persistence pays.* She began to stroke the shaft as she worked the thickness farther into her mouth and throat, then wrapped her lips and sucked. Salty and a bit sweet. She reached under and grasped the skin covering his balls. She pulled gently. Was he one of those men who enjoyed that?

"Oh shit. That feels so damned good."

Bingo. His hips were starting to buck big-time, and she grasped his butt to hold him down. Though she could never have held him for real, he let her control the moment and backed off, keeping his hips almost still as she deep throated as much as she could take. The feel of him in her mouth was heaven. Big, fat, and juicy. She licked and sucked as his moans and cries got louder.

Then she popped her mouth off. "Want you in me, *cheri*. Have you got lube? Condoms?"

He waved toward his jeans. Had he brought the supplies for her, or were they left over from the gay bar? Did she care? Hell no. She scooted to the edge of the bed, grabbed the jeans, and rifled the pockets. Pay dirt. With a packet of lube and condom in hand, she pushed back so she was sitting between his long, muscled thighs. He was pumping his cock with his big hand, and the sight almost took her over the edge.

"Let me." She took over pumping and fitted the condom on with her other hand. Lube came next, on his cock. She smiled at him. "Want to lube me?"

He looked uncertain.

"No problem. I'll do it."

She generously lubed her hole and concentrated on relaxing. Just staring at that waiting penis made her stomach clench with need. It had been a while.

After she was well lubed, she raised herself up on her knees and scooted forward. His eyes widened. She leaned down and brought her lips to his. His mouth was a little dry, probably from anxiety, but his cock was rock hard. Good. That was all she needed.

He whispered, "I don't mind being in your pussy. You don't have to ass fuck."

She licked his ear. "Are you kidding? I love it. Don't worry, bebe; this is what I want. Now give it to me."

She rose up, positioned his big rod at her hole, and staring into those bright blue eyes, she began to lower her body. At first she thought the ring of muscle wouldn't release, but with a little concentration, she relaxed, and his cock began to slide in like a spoon through butter. Holy *merde*, burn much? She kept lowering, knowing the moment of pleasure was coming. When he was seated deep, she thought his eyes would pop from his head. "Feel good, bebe?"

"Oh shit, yes."

"Good, to me too." And that was finally true. Her muscles molded to his dick, and her whole body began to sing as the nerve endings got stimulated. She rose and then slowly fell.

He threw his head back. "Jeeezus, I knew that ass was magic."

She did it again, and then, locking her thighs, she began to ride him like a great, beautiful palomino. Up and down. He was actively helping now, thrusting his hips up as she descended. She reached down with one hand and began to massage her clit.

"Let me." He brushed her hand aside and began to stroke in small circles over the swollen bud. "Is that okay? Am I on the right spot?"

Little flames streaked into her womb. She loved that he cared. Mitchell hadn't given a damn that she even had a clit. "Yeah, it's perfect."

That big cock in her ass stoked nerves she hadn't ever felt before. His big, flat thumb on her clit hit all the right notes. Like his uncertainty kept him from pushing too hard and made it just right. *What a ride.* She could get addicted. *Merde.* Up and down, a little around, up and down. Hot, hotter.

Going to come. She didn't want to go alone, but in a second, she wouldn't have a choice. Then his massaging fingers faltered, and his head flew back again on the pillow. "Oh crap… I'm gonna come. Shit, yes…"

She put her hand over his and rubbed her clit with his fingers as his hips bucked uncontrollably. "Oh shiiiiiiit."

Flash. Her nerves expanded in a wave of heat that filled her whole body and blackened her vision. *Sooooo good. So good.* And she came and came.

Angel collapsed over his chest and listened to his heart beat fast. She'd just had incredible sex with a gay man. What the hell did that mean for her? More importantly, what did that mean for him?

Chapter Seven

The first thing she knew was this wasn't Africa. Way too comfortable and cool. The second thing she knew was that she was alone. Sniff. Sheets smelled like sex and Cal. Stretch. Nobody. She sat up and looked around the beautiful blue and gray room. No jeans or T-shirt on the floor, no light in the bathroom. There was light coming from behind the drapes, however, so it must be morning. And how exactly was she going to find her gay boy this morning? Freaked? Happy? Better go find out.

As she got up, her butt reminded her of a pretty spectacular evening. She hit the shower, smiling at the memory of Cal's face when he saw her naked parts that first time. How had her girlie bits affected him last night? She didn't want to hope for too much. Hell, he was gay. Gay guys would tell her she had plenty of heterosexual men to choose from. Stop fishing in their pond. And that would be fair. But she really couldn't control the feelings. Maybe it was the very gayness that gave his alpha male appearance and persona that generous, unsure, sensitive edge. She had a domme streak, and she couldn't resist him.

Clean, with her short hair wet and hand combed, she dressed in her favorite baggy jeans and a long-sleeved T-shirt. Scuffing her slippered feet, she went out of the room and down the stairs toward the sound of the TV. As she approached the great room, she heard the announcer talking about somebody named Dante. She wasn't sure if that was the first name or last. Apparently he was some big money man who contributed to a lot of charities and was buying a large interest in some New York soccer team. She heard the name of Global Outreach mentioned in the list of charities he supported, and that perked up her ears. Must be a decent man, because she thought her organization did a hell of a lot of good.

Caleb was half lying on the big sectional, one arm over the back, one leg on the seat. He seemed really interested in the story.

"Good morning."

He turned toward her and blushed scarlet. Very cute, but probably not a good sign. "Hi."

She gestured toward the TV. "Interesting story?"

"Yeah. This guy put a bunch of money into the Rocket Dogs."

"Oh, the football team?" She remembered they called it soccer in the US.

"Yeah, do you like football?"

"It's huge in Senegal, so it's hard to escape." She rounded the end of the couch and sat a few feet from him. "Is that your team?

"Yeah, I'm the goalie for the Rocket Dogs."

"They're pretty good. No wonder you've got such a great body."

He blushed again. Yep, not good. She rushed on. "So this guy putting in money must be good for you?"

"Well, sort of. Except I have to figure out if I want to sign a contract soon, and he's gonna be one more bigwig pushing me, I imagine."

"Don't do what you don't want to do."

He ran his fingers through that shot-gold brown hair. "I wish I knew what that was."

That seemed a good enough lead-in. "So was last night something you shouldn't have done?"

He paused, turned off the TV, and stared at her. "No. I'm glad I did it. We did it." There was the blush again. "Just not certain why."

"Well, mon grand, I seem to recall a pretty spectacular orgasm…"

"Whoa. Don't get me wrong, Angel. I loved it. It was great. I really want to do it again. It's just I wish I knew why I suddenly went ape shit for a woman."

She was still back on *"I want to do it again."* She had to catch up with his thinking processes before she could answer. "Uh, first let me say I loved it too, and I also want to do it again."

Blush. Okay, maybe not so bad this time.

She scooted closer to him on the couch, took his arm, and put it around her shoulders. Then she leaned against that hard, hard body. "Okay, let's explore your diversion."

He gave her a little kiss on her hair. "Okay, well, we already said it has something to do with you looking like a boy. Even nude you're boyish, but hell, you sure are cute."

She looked up at him. "Thank you, mon grand."

"What does that mean?"

"It's an endearment that means something like 'my big guy.'"

He got quiet.

"Don't you like it?"

"It's not that. It's just, that was what he called me…Elijah. My one-nighter."

"You know, I've got a bit of a theory about that too."

"What do you mean?"

"We said you like that I'm boyish, but I also think you like that I'm not a boy."

"Why would that be true?"

"Because then I don't have to be like him. What's his name? Elijah?"

"You think I'm that messed up by him?"

"You mean so messed up that you'd turn to a girl?" She smiled.

"No, you know what I mean."

"I think he had an impact."

"Yeah." He pulled her closer. "But so have you."

"Are you hungry?"

"Is that French for horny?"

"Merde, I hope so. Where are your condoms and lube?"

He reached in his pocket.

"Are you some kind of Boy Scout, always prepared?"

"Something like that."

"But we probably don't want to wreck this gorgeous couch."

"I happen to know this couch is washable, because its three owners are about as randy as they come. They've probably fucked on every available surface in this house. Sorry, didn't mean to give you too much information about your cousin."

"Are you kidding? She's Shakti's daughter, and Shakti didn't raise any prudes. Plus, I've seen pictures of her lovers. Yum-my."

"I hope that yumminess runs in the family." That grin could only be called *cat eating canary*.

"Are you kidding? Get that cock out, mon grand, and let me go to town on it."

"How 'bout you let me do the going to town this time?" He pushed her down flat on her back. After that alpha move, he looked a little less certain. "Remember, it's been a while for me…"

She nuzzled his ear. "Don't worry; I'll help."

He pulled off his sweatpants, and she was delighted to see no underwear and Monsieur Cock at full attention already. He had been planning this. He turned attention to rapid removal of her baggy jeans, and she helped by pulling off the T-shirt. She never wore a bra. What was there to contain? Ripping the condom wrapper with his teeth, he grabbed the rubber and fit it on the swollen dick. The reservoir was already wet from his precum.

She reached for the lube, but he stopped her. "I thought I'd put this in the designated scoring zone."

"You sure? I know you like my butt."

"I love your butt, but I want to know what you feel like. Okay?"

"Hell yes."

"Uh, do you need the lube there?" He vaguely gestured to her vagina.

"No, cheri. I am dripping for that cock."

His cheeks colored a little, but he set to his task. Carefully positioning *le grand* penis at her opening, he pushed with careful intent.

For a moment, she was amused at his earnestness, then…oh shit, did that feel good. She loved anal sex, but feeling that big, hot rod in her sadly underused vagina was indescribable, it was so delicious. Mitchell hadn't been nearly this big, and she knew immediately that this was a new addiction. *Mes amies*, big cocks were *magnifique*.

He gazed in her eyes. Maybe looking for a little affirmation?

She gave him her best smile. "Bebe, you are great. Just fuck me senseless."

He accepted the command. His hips began to thrust as he held his lean, strong upper body on his straight arms to keep from crushing her. It was fun, because she could see his hips working between their bodies and pictured that beautiful penis ramming in and out of her. The position also put his pubic bone hard against her clit -- yes, just the way she liked it. *Mon dieu, good. Good. Oh, merde, so goooood.* She gazed at him, his blue eyes at half-mast. "I'm going to have to come, cheri. But don't worry. Take your time. I can come all daynight…shit!" She knew her eyes must have rolled back, and then all she saw was stars as molten heat shot through her.

His cries echoed hers. "Crap, it's great, oh crap…" And his body stiffened and his pumping got random, while his upper body shuddered. He collapsed, and she got to experience what over two hundred pounds of deadweight felt like. It felt great.

* * * * *

The warm water ran down Cal's back as he leaned one arm against the wall. Maybe it would wash away his confusion. Angel was down there making them breakfast. Angel. His Angel, he guessed. He hadn't even minded fucking her pussy. Hell, minded?

64

He'd loved it. The other girls he'd fucked when he was younger had been okay, but he had never missed the experience. Somehow this was just different. But what did it mean? Was he het now? Would he quit having sex with guys? Whew. Hell no. He couldn't imagine that. But he'd been so uninterested in those guys at the bar, and obviously very interested in his cute little boy-girl.

And what about Eli? *Shit, get over it, idiot.* That's what it was. A big fat nothing. He should learn from it and move on. He had bigger problems trying to figure out what he was going to do about being suddenly straight. *Wish Jake was here.* He'd had trouble reconciling his love for a man, but he'd worked it out. Of course, he'd gotten to have both his guy and his girl eventually.

Enough wasted water. He turned off the shower, got dressed, and went down to another of Angel's meals. This he could *so* get used to. Scrambled eggs with some kind of cheese and tomatoes, plus turkey bacon and some croissants were laid out on the big island bar. He grabbed a stool.

She put a croissant on his plate. "I found them frozen and heated them up." She served coffee with heavy cream -- she called it café crème -- and then joined him on a bar stool.

They'd been munching and chatting for a few minutes companionably when a phone rang. Shit, his cell. He'd kind of forgotten what it sounded like the last couple of days. Roan had called once to check in, but he'd used the house phone. "Excuse me."

He left the kitchen and found his cell in the great room where he'd stashed it before they'd had sex. Yeah. Great sex. He hit green. "Martin."

"Hey. Cal. It's Whitaker."

"Hi, Mr. Whitaker." The owner of the Dogs. Damn, Cal had hoped for some more time.

"Hey, kid, can you come into the city for a meeting tomorrow morning? I've got someone I want you to meet."

Hell, he knew who. "Dante?"

"Yeah, you been watching the news? You're supposed to be on vacation."

He didn't say *some vacation, with a meeting in the middle of it.* "What time?"

"Nine."

Shit. That meant he should probably leave this afternoon and stay at his apartment so he'd make it on time. He tried not to sigh. "Okay. I'll be there."

"Not a firing squad, kid. Dante's great. Very, uh, motivated."

Yeah, that was a euphemism for pushy. "No problem. I'll see you there."

He hung up and went back to where Angel was clearing their plates. "Let me help." He grabbed dishes from the island.

"Bad news?"

"Obvious, huh?"

"Let's say you look a lot more serious than you did about an hour ago."

He kissed her neck in passing. "Oh, I don't know. I thought I was pretty seriously good at that."

"Aren't we full of ourselves, monsieur gay man? But yeah, I agree. Want to tell me about the phone call?"

"I have to go into the city for a meeting tomorrow morning. Just like I thought, it's with this guy Dante. Anyway, I should leave this afternoon to get there early enough."

She looked down. "Oh damn."

"Yeah. But I'll come straight back, I promise. It does mean you'll have to do a little overseeing of the construction. Is that okay?"

"Sure. I build stuff in Africa all the time. Have to."

"Well, tomorrow a new subcontractor comes on. The finish carpenter. Maybe more than one. The head guy's name is, uh…" He walked over to a kitchen drawer and pulled out the note Roan had left him. "His name is Edward Daniels. The contractor says he's a last-minute replacement for some guy who was tied up on another job. This guy is supposed to be good. Comes highly recommended, I guess, so I don't imagine it will take much overseeing. Just welcome him, make sure he knows he can come to you with questions. I'll show you all the plans before I go."

"Okay. No problem." She still looked disappointed, which made him ridiculously proud. "Can I help you pack?"

"Pack? Hell, no. You can take my mind off the stupid meeting." He pulled a condom pack out of his pocket and crinkled it in his fingers. "Beat you upstairs."

They were both the winner.

Chapter Eight

Deep breath. Caleb exited the elevator directly into the reception area of Dante Global Enterprises. No cozy meetings in the team headquarters for this bigwig. A sleek, chic, and very pretty brunette receptionist, maybe a bit Asian, sat behind an ultramodern maple desk with stainless steel legs, the smooth top marked only by an outer-space-looking phone and a paper-thin laptop. To the side, some minimalist leather chairs and a glass table sporting one orchid gave Cal scant welcome or comfort.

"May I help you, sir?"

Yep, in his gray suit and red tie, he even qualified as a "sir." "Yes, please. I'm Caleb Martin. I'm here to see, uh, Mr. Dante and Mr. Whitaker." At least he hoped Whitaker would be there. The owner wouldn't throw Cal to this wolf alone -- would he?

The woman gave him a huge, professional smile. "Of course, Mr. Martin. They are both looking forward to seeing you. Let me take you back." She signaled to another woman in a glass cubicle to the side of the reception room. The woman, also brunette and attractive, came and took the receptionist's place as the woman led Cal down a polished wood hallway, passing glass-fronted offices all neat as a pin. Did anybody work here?

They arrived at double doors made of some exotic patterned wood, and the receptionist opened it, stepping aside for him. Cal walked into a huge, utterly austere room dominated by a wall of glass, showing the spectacular view of New York City from the seventy-first floor.

"Cal, welcome. Glad you could come." Whitaker, big, burly, and white-haired, rose from a comfortable-looking guest chair in front of a huge desk made mostly of maple, metal, and glass. He smiled paternally, as if this hadn't been a command performance for Cal.

Behind the desk, in front of a beautiful stone wall with water trickling down it, sat the man Cal recognized as Dante. The man rose slowly as Cal crossed to shake hands with Whitaker.

"Good to see you, sir." Cal smiled at the man who had hired him, but all his attention was on Dante.

The first thing you noticed on Dante was the striking golden yellow hair cut short against his head. The texture suggested that if it was allowed to grow, it would curl. But once you got past the hair, the eyes were it. Brilliant, commanding, and so light that his pupils seemed to stand out like black stones in clear water.

"Hello, Mr. Martin. I'm Elias Dante." He had a distinctive, high, slightly nasal voice. He walked around the desk and extended a hand. Cal shook it. Dante wasn't a large man, but he did fill up a space.

"I'm pleased to meet you, sir."

Dante gracefully gestured toward a couch and chairs in front of a small steel firebox set in the stone wall. Fire and water. Cal walked with Whitaker to the grouping and sat in one of the chairs. Whitaker settled back on the burgundy-colored couch. Dante went to a cabinet and unfastened it to reveal a full bar and refrigerator. "What can I get you?"

"Do you have beer?"

"Any kind you like, probably."

"Why don't you pick something for me?"

Dante raised golden brows. "Ah. Wise."

He brought Cal a bottle and glass. Cal looked at the Japanese label he'd never seen before. He poured and took a sip under Dante's watchful gaze. "Um. Really good." And he meant it.

Whitaker leaned back, hail-fellow-well-met. "So, Cal, how's the vacation going?"

"Well, thank you."

Dante leaned forward, sipping a glass of sparkling water he'd carried from the desk. "You must not have gone far to be able to join us today."

"No, I was in Connecticut at my brother's place."

"The scientist?"

Had Whitaker said something, or had Dante investigated? Cal couldn't help smiling at the earful a background checker would give Dante on Cal's brother's living arrangements. "Yes, that's right."

"So you must be looking forward to the new season."

Cal couldn't help but pause. That was a "when did you stop beating your wife" question if he ever heard one. What could he say? "Yes, I love soccer." And he knew that was the truth. He just didn't know if he wanted to spend his life as a professional soccer player.

"That's good, Cal, because Earl here and I feel you're very important to the team."

"Thank you."

"We got to see your talent on display at the end of the season, and we're hoping to see a lot more of it next year."

Cal stayed quiet for an uncomfortable moment. Whitaker knew Cal wanted time to think, and he'd let this ambush happen. Let him stew. The older man rushed into the silence. "Cal, Elias has invested a lot in the team."

"I'm aware of that."

Dante leaned forward. "And I'm a man who likes to protect his investments. You are an obvious talent, and we want to both secure and reward that talent."

Cal stayed quiet.

"We have a contract for you to sign. A generous contract."

"Thank you, sir. I'll look forward to reviewing and considering it."

"I'm sure when you see the terms, there will be nothing to consider, aside from the legalities, of course. You'll want your lawyer to review it."

"Yes, I'll be happy to do that right after I've thought about it."

"What is there to think about?"

Cal looked at Whitaker, who had the grace to look embarrassed. "Mr. Whitaker knows that I have thought about a different kind of future."

"This career is every young man's dream. What kind of future would you consider to top it?"

Cal shifted and sipped his beer. "I have a degree in sociology. I've thought about graduate school, teaching, perhaps working directly with the homeless..." Yeah, he was rambling. That was because he didn't know what he wanted to do. Why couldn't this just be easy? He couldn't get settled on the idea of soccer as his life's work, but his drive toward something new wasn't as strong as his pull away from what he had. It made him wishy-washy. Crap, he hated it.

Dante flicked a hand impatiently. "Yes, yes, there will be more than enough time for such things when your soccer career is over. Meanwhile, you'll have enough money to help people, support your family, give to your brother's charity."

Cal leaned forward toward Dante. "Neither my family nor my brother is interested in my support, sir. They want me to do what I want to do."

Whitaker interrupted. "Yes, Cal, and so do we."

Dante smiled. "Actually, we want you to be starting goalie next season."

What the -- "Morales is starting goalie."

"Yes, and Morales is injured."

"He's recovering rapidly. I saw him just before I went to Connecticut. He's going to be fine and is crazy to get back on the field."

"The simple truth is that Morales isn't as good as you."

Cal stared at Dante like he was a snake. Morales was a friend. He had a family. "That's debatable. And I assure you, I'm not taking another man's position because of some imagined margin of talent.

Morales is a great goalie. He's earned his position, and I won't take it from him."

Whitaker leaped in. "Of course, Cal. Elias simply means if Morales doesn't recover or can't play for some reason."

Cal sat back, eyeing them both. The two men exchanged a look. *Yeah, buddy, back off.* Dante got the message. "Cal, we want you to be happy with the team. The reason for this meeting was just for me to be able to tell you how important you are to the Rocket Dogs…and to me personally, as an investor in the team. We'll have the contract sent over to you at your brother's home, if you'll leave the information with Michelle at the front."

Cal started to rise. Whitaker stopped him. "One more thing. Since you're in town anyway, I wonder if you could stay over and do a media event tomorrow? I know it's an imposition, Cal."

Shit, he *so* didn't want to stay and do press stuff. "Okay, sir. Where and what time?"

After getting the details and saying good-bye, it took him a few more minutes to get the hell out of Dante Global Enterprises. Dante. Good name. Reminded Cal of some circle of hell. When he emerged on the street, he hit Send on his cell phone.

"This is Angel."

"Hi. It's me."

"Hi, mon grand. How was the meeting?"

"Just as bad as I expected, plus I've got to stay over another night for some press crap tomorrow. Sorry."

"Well, merde. They shouldn't be taking away your vacation."

"Tell me about it."

"Plus, I kind of miss you."

There was that stupid pride thing again. He could make a girl miss him. Strange values he had. "Me too."

"Oh well, I'll keep busy. I saw some new workers in the back, so I'm about to go out and check on things and introduce myself."

"Great. Thanks so much for doing this, Angel."

"Hey, no problem. Alpha males with leather and steel on their butts. What's not to like?" She laughed. "Just kidding, cheri. Get home as soon as you can."

"Yeah. Home."

He hung up and walked toward the subway that would take him to the apartment. It'd been strange staying in the crowded, messy place with two guys last night after the beauty, space, and quiet of the Connecticut home.

He'd been on vacation almost a week. Sure as hell didn't feel much closer to a decision about his life. Of course, there had been a few unexpected distractions. Yeah, distractions of various sexes.

He descended the steep, dirty stairs into the subway. He hadn't liked Dante much, but the guy was really just a financial wolf looking out for his own best interests like they all did. Cal didn't have to love him to play for him.

What the man said about the money made sense too. Hell, most people would tell Cal he was an idiot to even think of walking away from the potential of millions. But the Martins had never really gone after money. Other things had always been more important. Probably he could help people more if he had the dollars to do it with, and he could go save the world later. He sighed as he brushed past the rushing New Yorkers on the subway platform. But the press and the groupies and the constant notoriety? Crap, he sure wasn't shy, but he hated all that attention and the pretending he was somebody else. Someone he wasn't. And for five years -- or more? He sighed again as the train rushed into the station, taking his breath. What the hell did he want?

* * * * *

Angel caught a glimpse of a person disappearing into the guesthouse as she walked across the lawn toward the construction site. Wow, golden hair. She looked at the nearly completed structure in front of her. This guesthouse was bigger than a lot of people's homes. In Senegal, it would have been a mansion. It was modern and sleek like the main house, and she loved how it nestled into a softly rising hill on the back of the property. All the drywall was apparently complete, and the exterior of the house was just awaiting finishes like stone and glass. So it must be time for woodworking and cabinetry.

She saw Randy, the project boss, up on the roof, but not the contractor she'd met the day before. She waved. "Hi, just going in to meet the cabinetmaker."

He waved back.

She entered the building through the entry and then crossed into an open space that would soon be a compact living room. Like in the big house, the living and dining spaces were separated from the kitchen by an island/breakfast-bar combo, still waiting for its granite countertop.

In the still-raw kitchen, she saw a man she hadn't met. Must be the new guy. He had his back turned, and she got a look at golden wheat-colored hair pulled back in a tight queue at his neck. He was medium tall and quite slim, with long legs, but the arms sticking out of a construction vest looked capable.

"Mr. Daniels?" He turned, and she almost gasped. What a gorgeous face. Not one you saw every day. Movie-star beautiful, but maybe the star in question would be more Marilyn Monroe than Clark Gable.

To cover her amazement, she stuck out her hand. "Hi, I'm Angel Silvay."

He cocked his head as if giving her a quick once-over, then shook her hand. "I'm Edward. Um, I was told I should ask for Dr. Martin or Mr. Black…"

"Oh, I'm sorry. I thought the contractor would have talked to you."

"No, I haven't seen him."

"No problem. Mr. Black and Dr. Martin and, uh, Dr. Silvay went on a last-minute vacation. Dr. Martin's brother was supposed to be here to meet you, but he got called into the city, and I'm Dr. Silvay's cousin and…shit, this is complicated to explain. Bottom line is, I can answer your questions or find somebody who can, okay?" She laughed.

He smiled back, and that was an awesome experience. Dimples, white teeth, and really unusual eyes. Something about Cal's description of "the guy" came back to her. What were the chances there were two such androgynous men? But this guy was Edward and that wasn't the name Cal had said, she was pretty sure. Man, if this was the guy, she sure as hell could understand the attraction. Of course, it would also mean he was gay.

He was staring at her. "I hope you won't take this the wrong way, but…"

"Yes, I'm a woman."

He grinned and shook his head. "Of course, you must get that all the time. No offense. You sure are pretty."

"So are you, and you're a man, right?"

He shrugged. "Let's hear it for androgyny."

Okay, enough flirting. After all, there was Cal, and she missed the big guy. "Anyway, do you know what's happening in here, or should I call the contractor?"

He pointed to some big sheets of paper lying on a worktable. "These seem to be pretty complete." He flipped through. "I think I'm working on kitchen and bathroom cabinetry and" -- he turned to another page -- "this entertainment wall in the living room." He grinned. "That will be fun." He looked around the space where boxes of preconstructed cabinets plus piles of wood were stacked. "Looks like all the materials are here."

She handed him a sticky note. "Here's the house phone number if you need me, or come up to the French doors and knock. I'm usually around."

He took the note and gave her a mischievous grin. "I like it when a pretty girl gives me her number."

So, he wasn't gay. "Don't get cocky, pretty boy." She smiled and left, walking back up to the house through the cold, damp grass. The autumn colors had really taken hold, and she took in the beautiful trees in red, orange, and gold as far as she could see. So different from Senegal. The house was quite isolated, the nearest neighbor barely visible beyond the trees. Roan must be one seriously rich boy.

Okay, assuming the traveling trio returned soon, there might be a baby in the offing. She'd found Em's doctor's number earlier. Time to call and touch base. She planned to deliver the baby at home, but she needed the doctor's cooperation and planning in case of emergency. That would help take her mind off cute blond guys she had no business thinking about.

Chapter Nine

"Will you be starting goalie next season, Cal?"

Cal shifted uncomfortably in front of the microphone. "No, Pedro Morales will start."

Whitaker grabbed the microphone in front of him. "Of course, that depends on Pedro's rapid recovery."

The army of press started shouting questions.

"How's he doing?"

"What do the doctors say?"

"Will his injury affect his game?"

Cal leaned forward and tried hard to smile. "I saw him a few days ago, and he's doing great. Should be good as new." Whitaker gave him a look, but Cal wasn't going to have the press believing Pedro had lost his edge with the shoulder injury. Goalies broke their shoulders all the time. His had been broken twice. Of course, not in multiple places like Pedro's.

"Hey, Cal, you got a girlfriend?" The shout came from the back of the room.

Well, hell. For once he could kind of tell the truth. "Actually I just met somebody. But she lives a long way away, so I don't know if we've got a future."

The voice was snide. "I heard you like guys more than girls."

Cal stood up to his full six feet five and smiled. "Yeah, buddy, I like guys just great." He bunched up a fist and raised it, he hoped, threateningly. "Why don't you come up here and let me show you how much." It was an alpha-male nonanswer, but the kind the press loved, and most of the reporters howled and snapped photos

One of the female reporters stood up. "Hey, Cal, if your girlfriend isn't available, I'll be glad to dry your tears." And once again, Cal escaped a confrontation with the press unscathed.

Since he was standing, he started to gather his stuff while Whitaker thanked the press for coming. A couple of the other players stayed to answer one-on-one questions, but Cal walked off the dais and toward the rear exit.

The owner of the nasty voice stepped toward him. Cal recognized him as a reporter for a particularly unpleasant little gossip rag. The guy snarled. "You can't fool them forever, faggot."

Cal wanted to make a snappy comeback, or at least tell him to go to hell, but the guy would twist and print anything he said. No use giving him a bigger story. Plus, there was no arguing with the truth. Cal brushed by him and out the door.

When he hit the cool autumn air, he took a deep breath. The guy was right. The day was coming. That prick was just the vanguard of a whole army of press, and they'd all be dying to pull him out of the closet. It would be a relief to be out to the world, but the crap he'd get from the press and some of the other players would make that relief hollow. All sports were intolerant to gay players. Soccer was international. It was the worst.

Cal walked toward the train. His cell phone rang. Whitaker.

"Martin."

"Hi, Cal. You did good this morning, thanks."

"No problem." He dodged hurrying pedestrians as he got closer to Penn Station.

"Hey, were you serious about having a girlfriend?"

Well, shit.

When Cal didn't reply immediately, Whitaker rushed on. "I mean, no pressure, kid, but if it's true, it sure would make life easier for the team, you know? That guy today was nasty."

"Yeah, he was."

"So, you don't have to tell me about your love life or anything, but if it's true, I'll just say we're behind you, and me and the missus would love to meet her."

"She works in Africa, so I doubt that's going to happen."

"Shit, kid, you weren't kidding about the long-distance thing. But that's great, you know. Just great." He laughed. *Shit. Wish he wasn't so obvious about being happy he doesn't have to deal with a gay goalie.* "Thanks, Cal. Enjoy the rest of your vacation."

"Yeah, thanks." He hung up.

Thanks for nothing. Shit!

* * * * *

Angel got off the phone with the doctor and made a few more notes. If Em checked in with her MD, Angel's arrival would no longer be a surprise, but *c'est la vie.* Of course, Em knew she was coming sometime, just not that she'd arrived now. She needed to be prepared. It had taken the doc a day to get back to her, but after the call, she felt pretty satisfied that they were on the same page. Em had chosen a holistic MD who was sympathetic to midwifery and home birth, so no issue of the skepticism and outright anger she got from some physicians.

She padded toward the kitchen. Better go file these notes in the folders in her room.

She heard the tapping on the French doors. *Okay, don't get too excited.* It could be any of the construction guys. Just because she hadn't told any of the other men they could knock on the door didn't mean anything.

She saw the blond hair first, shining in the afternoon sun. It was hard to reconcile the tripping of her pulse at that sight with the little ache she had from missing Caleb. Weird. It had been a long time since she'd been attracted to one man, much less two. This one was probably just a pretty face. Very pretty.

79

She opened the door and leaned out. He was standing on the slate terrace, holding something in his hands. She couldn't help glancing at his strong, tan forearms, bare beneath the rolled-up sleeves of a T-shirt and vest. "Hi. Got a problem?"

He grinned. "Kind of. I just realized the cabinet and drawer pulls haven't been ordered, and I need to get that done quickly so they arrive on time. Got a minute to look at samples?"

Pitter-pat. "Sure, come on in." She led him to the big rough wood table in the dining area of the open living space. "I'm not sure I've got the expertise or the knowledge of the homeowner's tastes to make this selection. Drawer handles are kind of a big deal, aren't they?"

He didn't answer, and she turned to find him staring at the house's interior. "Beautiful, isn't it?"

"Yeah. Really nice. Just my taste."

"Well, that's good, because then maybe you can help pick the pulls." She continued on to the table and sat. He pulled out the opposite chair, then spread some handles out in front of her.

For the next half hour, they discussed the pros and cons of each set of pulls. He obviously had great taste, so she trusted his recommendation of brushed nickel handles shaped like zephyr wings. She smiled. "Want some tea or coffee?"

He looked up at her. Those eyes were gold. No other description. "Yeah, but I should order these things now."

"You can use the phone while I make the tea." She got up and went toward the kitchen as she heard him talking. Well, this was stupid, but he was fun to talk to. He seemed to know so much about all the materials and the style of the house, and he had an easy manner. Flirtatious too, which was more of a problem.

She started the automatic tea maker that had become her favorite thing in the kitchen. A quick hunt uncovered some lemon crisps. Yum. Roan loved good things.

"I placed the order."

She looked over her shoulder. He was standing by the island. "Take a seat. Tea coming right up." She put out cups and a plate of the cookies.

He settled on a stool. "Must say my tea party skills are a little rusty."

She glanced up. Was he making fun of her? "You certainly don't have to stay. Feel free to go back to work."

He cocked his head and gave a small smile. "Sorry, that came out wrong. I mean really, I'm not used to being around women that much. And I think you're so attractive. I just don't want to do the wrong thing."

That was sweet. She smiled back. "Would you rather have a beer?"

"No, actually I'm looking forward to the tea."

She poured into the cups. "It seems unlikely that you wouldn't be around women much."

"My work doesn't put me in contact with a lot of females."

She looked up. "There's after work."

"Yeah, well, I'm not too social with the ladies."

Odd wording. She thought of Cal. Could it be? "You don't live around here, the contractor said."

"I have a place up in the woods in Vermont."

She laughed. "No wonder you don't see a lot of ladies. Pretty remote living."

He looked into his cup as if he could read the tea leaves, then took a sip. "Good."

"You want milk in it? Lemon?" She'd put out the sugar, but he hadn't used it.

"No, thanks. So, do you live in this great place?"

"I wish." She shook her head. "No, actually I don't wish. I live in Senegal, in Africa. I work for a global organization that provides health care. I'm a midwife."

"No shit? Uh, sorry. No kidding?"

"Shit is fine by me, and I see a fair amount of it in my line of work."

He laughed. "What are you doing here? Vacation?"

"Kind of, but mostly I'm going to deliver my cousin's baby."

"No shit?"

Angel heard the front door open. Oh crap. She glanced at Edward. This might look weird to Cal. Hell, it *was* a little weird.

"Hey, Angel. I'm back." The call came from the entry.

Better face the music. "In here."

Edward turned on his stool just as Cal came around the corner into the great room. Cal stopped dead and stared at the carpenter.

For a moment, there was nothing. No movement, it felt like no breath. She laughed a little. "Cal, this is…" She looked at Edward, and the words died on her lips. The man was transfixed. A glance at Cal showed he was similarly mesmerized. Shit, maybe her guesses about the man had been correct.

Edward rose and walked slowly toward Cal. "Hello, Caleb."

Cal nodded. "Eli. What in the hell are you doing here?"

"I'm not sure."

So that was it. He was the one, the man who'd so thoroughly gotten under Caleb's skin.

She watched the smaller man stop in front of Caleb, and suddenly Cal reached out, grabbed his head, and pulled him into a kiss. Far from protesting, Edward…Eli…whoever…wrapped his arms around Cal and sucked his face like some elixir of immortality lay in Caleb's mouth.

She couldn't breathe. What had she thought? Not this. Two men. Gay men. Both men she wanted. One she'd had and wanted a lot more of. And it seemed couldn't have again. Merde. *C'mon, Angel, be cool.* Something inside went *crack* as she watched the two men, those beautiful men, kiss like they were searching for their souls. Tears pushed at the back of her eyes. No, she didn't own him. She couldn't feel this way. Couldn't act this way. She'd even been flirting with the other one. This was her payback, and it was a bitch. Then the sob escaped. *Oh shit.* And she ran straight for the stairs.

Chapter Ten

Having Eli's tongue in his mouth again felt like heaven. He wanted to keep it there forever. But damn, he wanted to know what the hell was going on even more.

Cal pulled his head back, feeling like he was recovering from some heavy drug. "Hang on. What the fuck is happening?" He looked at Eli. "Why are you here? How did you get here?" He raised his head and looked around. "Where's Angel?"

Eli leaned his forehead against Cal's chest. He sounded like he'd nearly drowned and needed life support. "I think she ran upstairs. I think she was upset."

"Shit."

"Why was she upset, Cal?" The gold eyes looked up at him.

"Hell no. I don't owe you any explanations, and I'm not doing this one-on-one. Come with me." Cal grabbed Eli's wrist. The guy might be strong, but Cal was stronger. So he got off when Eli dominated him in bed, but not now, buddy. Cal wanted some answers. He dragged Eli through the great room and up the stairs to the second level. A few doors down the hall, he stopped in front of Angel's room. The door was closed. He tried the handle. Locked. "Angel, it's me. Open the door."

From inside the room, he heard a muffled reply. "Go away. You have what you want."

"Women!" Fuck, he'd never expected to say that in his life. He banged on the door. "Angel, open the damned door, or I'll kick it down and ruin Roan's beautiful woodwork."

Eli leaned against the door. "And I'll have to fix it."

There was a pause, then a *click*, but the door didn't open. Cal pushed the handle down and shoved. Success. Angel had made it all the way back to her bed and was sitting, arms crossed over her chest, her back against the headboard, looking like a beautiful, sulky teenage boy.

Still holding Eli's wrist, Cal pointed to the other side of the bed. "Sit." He released him, and Eli did as he was told with a tiny, wry smile.

Okay, had to get out of this fucking suit before he did one more thing. He ripped at his tie and pulled it off, removed his suit coat, folded it over a chair, and kicked off his shoes. He glanced up to find gold eyes and brown ones gazing at him. Angel looked like she would gladly slit his throat, and Eli looked like the whole thing was damned funny. Neither said a word.

Let 'em wait. He took a few more minutes getting comfortable than he absolutely had to, then sat on the end of the bed opposite Eli, his body turned halfway toward each of them. "Nobody is leaving here until I know what's going on. Got it?" No response from the peanut gallery. He pointed at Eli. "You. You left me. I woke up, and you were gone. What the fuck did you think, I was going to try to drag you to a preacher or something?"

"Cal, I'm sorry…"

"I know, I know, relationship rhymes with commitment."

"Kind of. I can't explain completely. I have this really complicated life that's not good for anyone, and it makes it hard for me to get close to people." He'd been looking at his hands, and now he looked up, gold eyes shining. "But shit, Cal, I've missed you so bad. Every day I wake up thinking of you."

Cal couldn't decide if he wanted to throw himself at the man or throw something at him. There were too many more questions. "Is that why you're here? You looked for me?"

Eli looked down again. "No. I didn't even know your last name."

Angel chimed in. "And speaking of names, you said your name was Edward. How come he calls you Eli?"

"My professional name is Edward, but my real name is Elijah. Part of that complicated life."

Cal took over. "So if it wasn't to find me, why are you here? This can't be a coincidence."

"I agree, it looks really weird, but somehow it actually is a coincidence. I was in New York visiting, uh, family. A friend called me and told me there was a great gay bar in Brooklyn and he'd meet me there. You know the rest of that. The next day, I got a call from, uh, a family member saying there was a woodworking job up for grabs because some other guy had backed out due to scheduling. He gave me a number for your contractor, and the guy hired me based on referrals. What are the chances we'd meet both places? Shit, that is serious coincidence."

Cal had almost lost track of Angel until he heard her voice laced with sarcasm. "Well, that explains everything oh so neatly, except what the hell the two of you are doing sitting on my bed?"

She hadn't moved from her cross-armed posture, brown eyes glowering. Pieces started falling into place in Cal's brain. WTF? He pointed at Eli. "So you didn't even know I was going to be here, and yet I found you in the chummiest of conversations with Angel, who, despite all appearances, is a woman! What exactly were you doing?"

Eli grinned. "Flirting." He shrugged. "Just because I like guys doesn't mean I don't like girls too, and she's adorable."

Cal grumbled. "I know."

Eli frowned. "Yeah, you sure as hell must know for her to be so upset at us kissing. What do you two have going, my gay friend?"

Angel piped in. "We *were* lovers."

Instead of exploding as Cal expected, Eli laughed. "Well, look at you, you tricky bisexual devil."

It was Cal's turn to pout. "I never said I didn't like girls."

"When was the last time you had sex with a female, not counting Angel?"

"Umm, five years ago."

"So that doesn't exactly make you an ardent bisexual." The gold eyes focused on Angel, who was watching this whole exchange like a Ping-Pong game. "You do have your charms, little Angel."

She put hands on her hips, which looked funny, sitting cross-legged as she was. "If you two have finished airing your laundry, why don't you leave my room since, despite my charms, I seem to have outlived my usefulness to both of you." She looked brave, but the tears in her eyes made her a liar.

Cal looked at her. Shit. He wanted Eli, he was sure of that, but the idea of walking out of Angel's room made his stomach ache. Still, he didn't know what to say. He got up slowly from the bed and took a few steps toward the door.

"Hey, big guy, if you don't want her, I sure as hell do."

Cal spun on the man. "What the fuck, Eli? You kissed me."

"Yeah, well, I just know you better. I was working up to kissing her."

Angel leaned forward. "Excuse me?"

Eli ignored her.

Cal was going to kill the man. "What in the hell do you want from me?"

Eli gave him a level gaze. "Why don't you answer that?"

"You want sex. That's all you wanted then, and I don't imagine that's changed." Crap, why should that feel like a stab in his heart?

Eli looked down for a moment, then back at Cal. "That's not completely true. Hell yes, I want sex with you. I picked you, remember, out of a lot of choices. You are something special, and if circumstances were different, I might want more." He shrugged. "But it is what it is."

Cal sneered. "It's not me; it's you."

Angel gave a little snort.

Eli smiled. "Yes, but that doesn't mean we can't have sex."

Angel leaned forward. "Then get the hell out of my room."

Eli ignored her again. "What do you want, Cal?"

What did he want? Romance, white picket fences? How did that fit into his life? He shook his head. "I don't know."

"Do you want to walk out of here like Angel said?"

Never have Angel again? Never have Eli again? Cal shook his head.

"So…?"

A whisper was all he could manage. "I want you."

"Just me?"

"No, I want Angel too."

"How the hell does that work?" She threw a pillow but missed Cal's head by a mile. Not a great pitcher.

Eli smiled like a wolf that'd just cornered little Red. "How it works is that Cal takes off all those clothes, climbs on this bed, and proves just how bisexual he is while I fuck the hell out of his ass."

Sheee-it. That shut him up. A threesome? Could he do that? It just happened that he had some very good role models. And hadn't he just been envying Jake for having both his man and his woman?

"Excuse me. Do I have anything to say about this?" Angel had come up on her knees, so the hands on the hips worked a little better.

Eli stretched out on the bed and rested a hand on her leg. "If you prefer, I can fuck you and Cal can do me, but I just thought since you know him better…" His grin was pure, evil glee.

She started to laugh and kept laughing until she collapsed on the bed on her back. "Well, that's one way to solve the problem."

Eli shifted, and as Cal watched, the beautiful man leaned over the laughing girl and kissed her. Cal could almost feel her gasp, but then her arms went around that lean, hard body Cal remembered so well. His chest contracted. Jesus, was he jealous? Shit yes. But of whom? Eli or Angel? Maybe that answered his question. Yes yes yes.

It only took seconds to pull off the dress shirt, unfasten his suit pants, and pull them down. He felt a little shy, so he left the boxer briefs on. Watching them kiss might make him jealous, but it also gave him one hell of a boner.

He crawled onto the bed, and without breaking the kiss that was now accompanied by serious groping, Eli held out an arm, and Cal moved under it. Eli raised his head from Angel's. "Kiss her while I go to work on her pussy."

Didn't have to ask him twice. He closed his mouth over hers and passed his tongue slowly over her parted lips. Angel whimpered and devoured him. She sucked his tongue as far into her mouth as physics allowed. Man, his cock loved it. Crazy, he really loved kissing this girl. Her lips were soft, but not as soft as Eli's. The man's were more like a woman. And she had that great dominant streak. She moaned into his mouth. *Oh yeah.* Cal opened an eye. Eli had taken off her jeans and was deep into her pussy. Wow, he wanted to see this. Cal pulled back and let her howl. Eli held her thighs firmly, but her hips were twisting and trying to buck. She wanted closer to that mouth. Smart girl.

Cal couldn't stand it. He grabbed the loose jeans Eli wore and pulled them down. Jesus, the man loved commando. His beautiful pink cock leaped out of the denim. It knew what it wanted. So did Cal. He scooted under Eli, grasped that rod, and swallowed it whole. Equal time. *Mmm. Salty, musky, and delicious.* Cal fondled Eli's balls, and the man moaned, which must have produced a vibration because Angel just cried out louder.

He felt hands on his hips. Still sucking, he opened an eye and saw Angel pulling at his boxer briefs. He reached down one hand and helped her, pushing them over the huge lump of his cock. He twisted his hips closer to her mouth and she turned her head. *Ah, rewarded.* Angel lapped a questing tongue around the tip of his cock like a garter snake, licked a few times, then popped as much as she could handle inside her wide-open mouth.

Oh man, this was great. Who'd have thought? They made one another hotter and hotter. Had to explode soon.

Eli pulled back from Angel's pussy. "Wanna fuck. Got condoms?"

Hell yeah! Cal unfastened his lips from Eli's beautiful cock, pulled out from under Eli, hopped off the bed, and ran to his room, where he kept the condoms and lube. He held onto his penis to keep it from bobbing. When he got back, Eli and Angel had switched to sixty-nine and were still consuming each other. "Hey, I got the goods."

Still eating pussy, Eli stuck out an arm. Cal dropped the condoms in his hand. Angel was whimpering, but Eli rose up on his knees, ripped open one condom, and put it over his own cock. Cal's mouth watered as Eli ripped a second package and then crooked a finger at Cal. Hell, yeah. Cal scooted forward, and Eli fit the condom over his penis. The beautiful face came closer. He licked along Cal's lips. "Want to top me, big guy?"

"Shit, yeah."

"Let me get in her first."

Angel put both hands on her hips, which looked pretty damned funny since she was lying down with her legs spread. "Will one of you please fuck me?"

Eli laughed. "Bossy little critter, isn't she?"

"The bossiest."

"Okay, my little dominatrix, here's what you want." Eli pushed her legs up, and in one smooth move, slid that long cock right into her pussy. She was dripping with Eli's saliva. Watching these two fucking each other just about topped his sexiest sights of the century list. Sheee-it, he had to grab his cock to keep from coming.

Angel's legs wrapped around Eli, and her hips rose up to meet his thrusts. "Merde, *ma beaute*, you are just as good as I imagined."

"Been fantasizing about me, cutie?"

"From the moment I saw you."

Eli looked over at Cal. "You gonna voyeur there, big guy, or would you like to get that cock in my ass?"

Didn't have to ask him twice. Cal applied lube from a little packet to his straining dick, then reached over and inserted a slick finger in Eli's ass. "That what you had in mind, beautiful?"

Eli's eyes closed. "More. Give me more."

Eli's hips were a moving target. It was tough inserting fingers. He managed to get two in, pushed down close to the prostate, and got a howl for his trouble. "Quit playing and fuck me!"

Cal positioned himself behind Eli's thrusting ass and grabbed his hips to hold him steady, which got a mewl of protest from Angel. *Okay, baby. Here it comes.* That pink, tight hole looked way too small to accommodate it, but just like the proverbial hot knife through butter, his cock slid in. *Oh. My. God.* That ass was hot and tight.

Eli threw his head back, mouth open and curls flying. "Ride me. Ride me till I come."

A pleasure to obey. Cal slammed his big cock into Eli's smooth, hard butt. Sweet Jesus, that was good. They developed a rhythm. Eli pushed in as Cal pulled out, and then pushed back onto Cal's straining cock. Cal understood now why Em and her men loved being a threesome. Knowing that Eli's cock was buried deep in Angel while Cal was balls to ass inside him amped the experience higher than Cal had ever imagined. "Jesus, I never want this to end."

Angel gasped. "Sorry, mon grand, I'm really close to the edge. But don't worry; I can keep coming all night if you guys keep reaming me."

Eli growled. "Plan on it." Angel cried out, froze for a moment, and Cal watched her eyes roll up as she whimpered and shuddered. Eli started pumping like a mad fool. "That feels so good. Make me come."

Cal slammed his hips into the man as Eli went nuts. He was coming. His beautiful man was coming because of him. Him and

Angel. Cal pictured cum filling that condom. *Oh shit. Oh shit.* Heat flashed up his spine. Head coming off. Hot cum spurted out his cock into the tight heat of Eli. Sweet God, he hadn't known anything could ever be this good.

He felt Eli collapse onto Angel. No way he could add to the pile, or the little girl child would get squashed. He rolled to the side, pulling his softened dick out of Eli. Eli reached out an arm and gathered Cal into the huddle. Angel's soft breathing touched his cheek. He rested his head next to hers. Jesus, two lovers. Out of the frying pan. He smiled and drifted into a sweet, warm doze.

Chapter Eleven

Elijah opened his eyes. Dark. Yeah, but he felt about as good as a man could and still be legal. He grinned. Actually, was having sex with two other people legal in this state? In any state? And he knew that he was in a shitload of trouble.

Crap, he'd violated his mantra. Never get involved, never. He liked people. Even loved them sometimes. But it was way too dangerous for people to love him back. But here he was. The night he'd met Cal in that bar, he'd known then he should run. The man sucked him in. Big, beautiful, generous, and gentle in amazing ways that you'd never expect from his strong frame. Eli never knew he had a type. That was because he hadn't met Cal yet.

And then there was his little tomboy. Not technically little. Probably five feet eight or so, but little next to Cal. He'd turned around in that guesthouse and thought the world had just given him his own boy toy. But the boy had been a girl. Funny, he mostly liked guys. He knew that there were men who were *gay for you*. Straight guys that fall in love with one man. He grinned again. Maybe he and Cal were bisexual for her. Man, she sure did it for him. With that dominant streak that challenged him and made him hot.

He sighed. They made him wish for more, and that was bad. All those years he'd run from his fate, dodging and hiding. And he'd lost. So now he found a modicum of happiness in his simple life. He loved working with his hands, took pride -- too much pride, actually -- in his work and fulfilling his promises. Maybe because the rest of his life was promise-free and had to stay that way. He enjoyed his little house in the woods and teaching kids woodworking. It was what he had -- and all he got. There was no way to fit a gay relationship into that conservative, guarded life, much less a ménage. Besides, Cal and Angel had big lives, and they both had to get on with them. They couldn't fit him into their worlds any better than he could make them a part of his. So, there was nothing for it but to live for the moment and accept what they had. Hell, he was good at that.

He felt next to him. Yep, a big, nude body generating soft snores. He felt the other side. No little, lean, boyish body. Hmm. Where'd she go?

He slipped out of bed, stepping carefully. Let the big guy sleep. The clock said 8:15. That would be p.m. They'd slept a couple of hours since they'd run up those stairs. He looked down at the beautiful, boyish face. He should walk away from Caleb again. He rubbed his chest. Yeah, that pain at the thought wasn't indigestion.

He felt around on the floor for his clothes, slipped on his jeans and shirt, and walked toward the light shining around the door frame. Out in the wood-floored hall, he took a deep breath. Yum. Follow those smells and he'd find Angel. He headed down the stairs to the kitchen.

Music played from a hidden sound system, something upbeat and pop sounding. As he rounded the corner from the great room, he saw her bouncing around the kitchen to the music while she checked something in the oven.

"Oh man, that smells so good."

She turned and smiled. Ooh, she was lookin' good in the slim jeans and T-shirt. Very nice on the ass. "You finally woke up, sleepy one. I'm making some dinner, so you may want to go wake the other Frère Jacques."

"What smells so good? Must be fish."

"Sole almondine. I'm making it with some rice pilaf and brussels sprouts. You like?"

"Oh yeah. I live alone, and a lot of the time I don't bother to cook much. This sounds like heaven."

"I love to cook, and I don't get to do it much in Africa, so this is also heaven for me."

"Want me to set the table?"

"Sure. The plates are up there." She pointed to a cabinet, then went back to the stovetop.

He grabbed some plates and moved toward the big table that occupied one end of the great room "So who did you say you work for?"

"A nonprofit called Global Outreach. We supply health care to third-world countries."

"Oh yeah, I've heard of them. I know someone who sup -- I mean, I've heard of them." Shit, he had to keep quiet. He wasn't used to talking to people.

He'd placed three plates and gone back for flatware. She glanced over her shoulder. "Why don't you go wake mon grand. Dinner's almost ready."

"Okay. I'll drag him up."

She gave him a smirk. "Make sure that's all you guys get *up*, or dinner will get cold."

He grinned and climbed the stairs. Had to be careful. This social interaction business was a minefield. He opened the bedroom door quietly, but Cal was already sitting on the edge of the bed looking a little bleary-eyed.

He went over and sat next to the big man. "Our little elf is down there making dinner."

"Yeah, I smelled it. Wait till you taste her cooking. Sheee-it, gourmet all the way."

Eli leaned in and kissed Cal's lips very gently. Sweet. One big hand came up to the back of his head and buried in his curls to pull him closer. He pulled back. "We've been warned that heads or other body parts will roll if we miss dinner."

"Yeah, she's passionate about her cooking."

"That's not the only thing. That critter can fuck."

"Yeah, I know. Makes me wonder if I've been missing something by not going bi all these years."

"I think it's just her. We're bi for her."

Cal laughed. "Okay, give me a minute to pee, and I'll be down."

"It's a deal."

An hour later, after consuming more food than he'd had at one time in years, Eli leaned back in his chair and sipped some sauvignon blanc. Man, he could get used to this. Not so much the lifestyle as the company. And that was the fucking problem.

Cal sipped his own wine. "Hey, Eli, you said you live in Vermont. So where are you staying?"

"I rented a place at an apartment hotel a few miles from here."

Angel came to the table carrying the most gorgeous fruit tart he'd seen. He touched a strawberry with his finger. "Tell me you didn't whip that up while Cal and I were sleeping. Hell, I'd have to marry you tonight."

She laughed as she cut. "Hold the preacher. It takes a bit longer to make tarts than I had. I found this in the second refrigerator. Roan must have left it for us."

"Left it for me, you mean." Cal extended a hand for the plate she passed. "He didn't know diddly about the two of you."

She passed a plate to Eli. "So, Cal, don't you think Eli would be more efficient if he stayed here? I mean, think how much work he can get done in the time he would have to drive."

Oh, *so* not a good idea. "Thanks for the thought, but I doubt Dr. Martin wants the hired help sleeping in his guest room. Plus, I expect work is the last thing that would get done."

Cal grinned. "You wouldn't be sleeping in the guest room. You'd be sleeping on top of me -- and Angel. I don't see how anyone could complain about such an efficient use of space."

Eli laughed but started clearing dishes. "Naw, I should get going. I'll see you in the morning anyway."

Crap, that was so true. If he was smart, he'd bail on this whole scene tonight. Shit, he didn't want to leave the work. There were so few things in his life to be proud of. He wanted to finish his job, do it right, feel good about it. It was important to him to finish what he started -- even if it only applied to carpentry.

They didn't say anything, but Eli turned in time to see Cal wink at Angel.

They finished clearing the table, and Eli put everything in the big dishwasher. Cal grabbed his hand. "C'mon. Let's watch a movie."

"Hey, remember that drive you were talking about? I should start making it."

"Just for a little while. C'mon."

What a weak-assed shit he was. He let himself be dragged into the great room. Angel turned off lights in the kitchen and followed with some beers in hand.

They settled on the big sectional side by side, and Cal pushed Play. The screen immediately came to life with two guys fucking. Shit.

Angel put her head in Eli's lap. "I requested this. I've never seen gay porn before."

"Ah, I see. This is an educational film."

"Yep."

Nobody said anything as the two guys on the screen moaned and gasped in best porn fashion. It was cheesy, but Eli's dick was still getting hard.

Angel flipped over on her stomach, leaning on her forearms. "I didn't get to see much earlier, but I think you two guys were much sexier than this phony movie. So why don't you two fuck, and I'll watch, and then I'll feel my education has been furthered."

Cal leaned over and kissed the side of Eli's neck. "Why don't we help the little lady, so she no longer has to suffer in ignorance?" Those lips became a soft, wet tongue, caressing his neck and moving toward his ear. Crap, how could he possibly be horny again? Easy answer. These two got him going with no effort. His body was hungry from too many lonely nights fucking his hand. But not tonight, sports fans.

Okay, big guy, my turn. He grabbed Cal and pulled him across his lap, then bent forward so his curls tickled Cal's nose. "What do you want? Tell me."

Cal laughed and twisted against the tickling hair, but his pupils dilated and his breathing got fast. Oh yeah, the boy had a big submissive streak, and he'd found himself two bossy doms. Eli grinned at his big boy trying to look all self-assured and sounding like a pleading girl. "I want your cock in my ass, Eli, as deep as you can get it. I want you to ram me until I scream and Angel is so turned on she comes just watching. Think you can do that for me, pretty boy?"

"You came to the right place." Eli ripped at Cal's sweatpants. "Let's see that big thing." He pulled them down below the pulsing, dripping cock. The guy was hot. "Angel, suck him while I get these clothes off."

She headed for that dick like it was better than the fruit tart. Cal moaned. Hell, who wouldn't with that pretty mouth all over you like a Shop-Vac? Eli pulled off his shirt and jeans. Man, these two were X-rated. Made that crap on TV look like a cheese factory. This was the real thing, and it made his cock hurt, he wanted to come so bad. "Hey, baby, time to turn him over. You want to lie under him and suck, or you want to watch?"

She popped the cock from her mouth. "Damn, I want both. I'll start out watching, since I didn't get to see much last time." She pointed at Eli's aching boner. "I really want to see that cock in his ass."

Eli grabbed Cal's shoulder. "Flip over."

Cal was instantly over and on his knees, butt stuck in the air and head on his hands. Angel leaned over and kissed that high, hard ass. "Bebe, you are so beautiful."

He'd second that. Eli pulled a condom on and lubed it up. "Angel, have you ever put your fingers in a guy's ass?"

"No." It was a squeak.

"Want to?"

"Hell, yeah."

He poured some lube into her hand and pointed to Cal's ready butt. Carefully, she pushed one slick finger into the tight hole. Her eyes widened as the pucker opened and let her in. She pushed the finger in farther. He wanted to laugh at her intense concentration. Then she grinned.

Eli shook his head. "He's pretty tight, 'cause he's been masquerading as a top all these years. Not enough cocks in his ass. But give him another one. He's ready."

She pushed in a second finger and really began to work them in and out. Cal was moaning and pushing back against her hand. She giggled. "I think he likes it."

"Watch this." Eli moved into position behind Cal.

She pulled her fingers out. Cal whimpered.

Eli laughed. "Don't worry; something even better is coming."

He positioned his cock against the well-lubed opening and pushed straight in.

"Sheee-it." The cry was muffled by the sofa cushions.

"You like that?" He began to ram. "Shame on you for pretending to be a top when all you wanted was to be fucked. But we're gonna make up for that, aren't we, baby? Your ass is getting what it needs now."

Cal's face was to the side, and he looked like he was almost crying. "Oh, yes. Please. Yes."

Angel was going nuts, grabbing her head, making mewling sounds. "Merde, you guys are so hot. I never dreamed how beautiful this could be. Oh God, that cock going into his ass. Give it to him, Eli. He loves it. Look how he loves it." Then she threw her head back. "Crap, I can't take it." She got down on her knees on the floor beside the couch, turned over onto her back on the couch edge, and slipped her head under Cal's body. Eli watched as she found that huge phallus, so ready to burst it was dripping like a fountain, and sucked the thing down.

"God. Shit, Angel, Eli. Shit, shit." Cal screamed, and Eli saw Angel's throat working. The man was coming like a fire hose.

Yeah, and he was so close he could practically taste the cum on the back of his throat. He pulled his cock out of Cal's ass, ripped off the condom, found another one where he'd tossed them on the table earlier. "Get over here, Angel. You're not getting left out of this."

She slid down onto the floor, ripped off her jeans. "*Oui*, s'il vous plait *por favor*, ma beaute, please, yes."

Cal was a collapsed heap on the couch, so Eli grabbed Angel under the arms and drew her up until she could kneel over his lap. "It's hot and ready, baby. Get it in you."

She grabbed his flaming erection, moved her hips forward, and lowered herself onto his cock with a deep moan.

He leaned forward and kissed her nose. "Get your clit against me tight. 'Cause I'm not gonna last long. Cal's ass is like heaven, and your pussy's just as hot. Ride hard."

Giddyap. Leaning forward so that her bud pressed hard against his pubic bones, she rode back and forth. "So good. So good. I almost came just watching you two. Mon dieu, if we ever need money, I'll rent you two out for gay porn. We'd make a fortune."

He chuckled. He was trying to hold off for another minute. Wanted her to catch up.

"Oui, Eli." Her rocking motion froze, and a soft keening sound escaped her lips.

Eli barely heard. Flash! Heat filled him as the cum rushed from his balls. Happy, happy balls. "Oh yeah. Oh yeah." His body shook like an earthquake victim as Angel collapsed in his arms. He didn't know about the future, but if he died right now, it would be as a happy man.

Chapter Twelve

Eli took another bite of omelet. *Mmm.* Feta cheese and tomatoes. The cutie could cook. How could anything this wrong feel so damned right?

He looked at Cal and Angel across the table, both absorbed in some online game they liked. They were playing on a tablet computer, Cal's fingers flying, and Angel watching over his shoulder. Heads bobbing, laughing, they looked really young, even though he knew Angel was actually older than he was. God, they were so damned adorable.

They had literally fucked one another's brains out last night. He may have protested, but he'd slept like the dead, with Angel draped over his back straight on till morning. He never slept with anybody if he could avoid it. Just like with Cal that first time, he got up and left while they were sleeping. And he never took anyone home. He went to their place, or he used a motel. Leave as few tracks as possible. This situation was a fucking minefield.

Plus, this whole setup felt weird. He made light of the coincidence to Cal, but the fact that he'd gotten a call to do this job right after meeting the big guy was damned suspicious. He should leave and go hide in Vermont, but he had a job to do. He was proud of his carpentry and wouldn't let a client down -- even to get himself out of deep trouble. "Hey, you guys, I need to get to work."

Cal made one last flying move, they both cheered, and then he set the computer aside. "Okay, pretty boy, do a good job, 'cause we're tough taskmasters. We'll think about you slaving while we're lying in the solarium."

Eli grinned. "Evil torturers."

Angel took his plate. "Seriously, sweetheart, is there anything we can do to help you?" She turned from the sink and waggled her eyebrows. "After all, we have a vested interest in getting you off work early."

"Thinking with your hormones again?"

"Always."

He gathered up his work vest from the side chair where he'd draped it earlier. "No, I'm good. I think I've got a guy helping me that the contractor assigned, so I should be fine…and fast." He smiled. "But I really have to go back to my apartment and change, or the crew is going to start to wonder if I ever shower or I just sleep in my clothes."

Cal looked up. "If you give us the key and directions, we can get your stuff, check you out, and move you in here."

Shit. What did he say? "Not sure how I feel about that in light of the rest of the crew. They'll notice for sure. Let me think about it."

Cal shrugged. "Okay. No pressure." That pretty face was trying to look matter-of-fact, but Eli knew disappointment when he saw it. Shit, he hated entanglements. But the kid was quick. Cal knew Eli was skittish about commitment, so he was backing off. Good. He'd leave it that way.

Angel piped in. "At least come up for some lunch. Cal is trying to make some decisions, and you could help. Just go around the front and come through that door."

"Okay, sure. See you later." Interesting.

Eli opted for the front door for his exit rather than plowing out the French doors. No use making too much of a statement to the other construction guys. He walked off the porch and around the side of the house on a stone pathway. If somebody noticed, they could think he'd parked his bike in front. As he started down the back lawn toward the guesthouse, his phone rang. Shit. Not many people called Eli. He was that reclusive.

He pressed the button. "Edward Daniels."

There was a slight pause; then he heard that familiar, slightly nasal voice he knew so well. "I suppose you have to perpetrate that fiction."

"Hello, Father."

"How is the job working out?"

Eli stopped walking. Okay, there was nothing inherently sinister in that question. "Fine, thanks."

"Good. So have you met the scientist, Dr. Martin?"

He just knew this was gonna be ugly. "No, he's on a vacation."

"Yes." Hmm. Odd response. "And have you met his brother?"

There it was. "Why would I have met his brother?"

"Come, Elijah, I know Martin's brother, Caleb, is house-sitting. And I know that you are, shall we say, intimately familiar with him?" The voice practically purred.

"Shit, Elias, what the hell is this about?"

"I did you a favor; now I want you to do me one."

"I never asked for this favor. Where do you come off setting me up so you can blackmail me?"

"There, there, Son. Harsh words. I not only got you a job I assumed you'd love, I also put you into the proximity of a man I know you must have found very attractive. After all, you didn't leave that motel room until daybreak. A new record in longevity for you."

Damn. Bad news delivered. He knew what the expression "bloodcurdled" meant. Yeah, his father had him watched, but he loved hiding his fucking head in the sand and pretending he was just a regular guy. Not somebody under surveillance. He hunkered down in Vermont and tried to act like he wasn't on twenty-four-hour Elias TV. Kid himself much? But where could he run? He'd hidden so many times. His father's reach was enormous. Sometimes Eli thought he was more ubiquitous than the CIA. Hell, he couldn't win.

"You're awfully quiet, Eli."

"So what the fuck do you want from me?"

"Nothing difficult. Not illegal, immoral, or fattening. Well, immoral…? Anyway, this afternoon, your lover is going to receive copies of some contracts. Before you think otherwise, they are excellent contracts that will set the boy up for life. All I want is for him to sign them, and I think you are in a position to nudge him in that direction."

"So why is it a problem? Why wouldn't he want to sign these contracts if they're as good as you say?"

"I don't know that he won't want to sign. You are my 'just in case' secret weapon."

"And why should I do this?" Crap, he already knew the answer.

The edge in the voice cut deeper. "You get to go on living your very private little life, without your clients and your students' parents knowing you're as gay as your pretty face implies, and without reporters knowing where, oh where, to find the prodigal son of the Dante empire. You get to go some more months doing whatever it is you do with those tools, not being forced into my business, not being asked for money by every leech in New England, going to gay bars and picking up unsuspecting young men without them ever knowing that they're fucking a billionaire's son. Does that seem fair?"

"Go to hell."

"Oh, and by the way, Eli. That lovely young woman who seems to be staying with Caleb, as well? She works for Global Outreach, one of my foundation's largest contributions each year. I'd say we cover a good fifty percent of their operating budget. I would hate to see what happened to that organization if their contributions from the Dante foundation were to be lost."

"You insufferable bastard."

The voice hardened even more. "And I'm sure there's a way for them to know that Ms. Silvay is the cause of their loss."

Crap, he'd already figured out the job was everything to Angel. And the organization seemed really worthwhile. He knew when he was done. "And if he signs, even if he was going to anyway, you'll leave Angel alone and won't withdraw your support?"

"Of course."

"And you'll leave me alone?"

"Yes, as much as I do now."

"You won't withdraw your watchdogs?"

His father chuckled. "Now why would I do that?"

"And if I try, but he still doesn't sign?"

There was a pause that gave Eli cold chills. "Just don't let that happen." The line went dead.

Eli crouched down and took some deep breaths. There was more to this than Elias was telling. He wanted to rush into the house and ask Cal what was going on, but he didn't dare. He didn't want anyone, even Cal and Angel, to know he was the son of Elias Dante. Shit, especially Cal and Angel. What would they think of a man with so little control of his own life he couldn't get out from under his father's thumb? They were both very grown-up. And he couldn't let something bad happen to Angel's organization.

He stood and headed toward the job. Maybe it would all be simple. Maybe Cal wanted to sign this contract, whatever the hell it was. Maybe Eli could just be happy for him. Yeah, maybe pigs wore the logo of American Airlines.

At lunch break, Eli had to fight the urge to get on the motorcycle and head north until he got lost in the Canadian wilderness. He'd tried it more than once, but Elias always found him. Waiting for the watchdog to show up on those occasions he'd escaped was almost worse than just living his life knowing they were there.

He got to the front door, squared his shoulders, and tried the handle. They'd left it open for him. Inside, he walked through the entry toward the faint sound of voices.

He called out, "Hey, where are you?"

Angel's voice answered. "In the dining room, Eli. Come on in."

He took off his work vest and tool belt and left them in the entry on the floor. As he approached the dining room, he saw both their heads bowed over something on the table in deep concentration. Another game? Then he saw the piles of papers. Shit. Here it was. "What's going on?"

Cal looked up. Yeah, and his face didn't look brimming with joy over how fucking great the contract was. Double shit. "Oh, hi. Just looking at this contract I got. I thought I might have a couple more weeks to make some decisions, but nope, gotta decide quickly."

Eli sat in a dining chair across from Cal. Angel brought him a sandwich and a glass of iced tea. "Thanks." He took a bite. "What's the contract?"

Man, he hardly ever saw Cal frown. "It's a five-year contract to play with the New York Rocket Dogs."

"Soccer, right?" Eli knew it was, but what the hell?

"You knew that's what I did for a living, right?"

"I heard someone say it in the bar that night." He chewed and swallowed.

"Yeah, that's what I do, and I signed a short-term agreement for part of this past season to be a reserve goalie. The first-string guy got injured, and I ended up playing a lot. I guess they liked it, 'cause now they want me to sign this big contract for five years."

Eli smiled. Yeah, crocodile that he was. "So what's the problem? Isn't it a good contract? They trying to shortchange you or something?" He finished half his turkey on wheat.

Cal shook his head like a whipped pup. "No, nothing like that." He looked up from under his lashes with those big blue eyes. "How much do you know about soccer, aka football?"

"Not much, really."

"But you know it's big all over the world. Much bigger than here in the States, right?"

"Sure."

"Can you imagine what it would be like to be a gay athlete playing the most popular sport in, say, Ireland, Argentina, the Middle East?"

Yeah, it'd be hell, and Eli would detest it. "Sounds like those guys need some lessons in diversity to me."

Cal grimaced a little. "But it's not me that gets the worst of it. It's the team. I've seen it happen with other guys. Their teammates get harassed for being in the locker room with a pouf, a fag. Even the gate gets affected, because some fans boycott the team to teach them a lesson." He sighed. "That's why, if I sign this contract, I have to stay in the closet, or try to, for another five years."

"You mean nobody on your team knows?"

"I told the owner and my roommates. They're okay with it, but the owner would rather he didn't have to deal with it, I know that. Plus some members of the press have wind of the story. They could make it hell for everybody."

"Living well is the best revenge." Cal glanced at him. Damn those puppy-dog eyes. Shit. He so wanted out of this mess. He took the last bite of his sandwich. *When you don't know what to say, chew.*

Angel came around the table. "But that's not the only reason Cal has doubts about the contract." She grabbed his empty plate. "Tell him, Cal."

The big guy stared down at his hands. "It's stupid, I guess." He glanced up, then back down. "It's just that I always wanted to do something important with my life."

"And being a big, rich soccer star isn't important?" Eli felt like a heel. Hadn't he spent his life trying to live his way, not using any of his father's money? And now he was suggesting that Cal should dance to his father's tune. Crap, he wanted to vomit.

"Well, my dad is a fireman. You know, he saves lives and property. And mom's a nurse. She's in her fifties, but she still goes in and works nights and double shifts because they don't have enough nurses. My sister runs this big charity, and Jake's helping save lives with his research. Hell, Angel gives her whole life to help people." He sat back, looking really defeated, and Eli's heart ached. "I guess I want to do something like that. But all I seem to be good at is throwing myself at a stupid ball."

Angel gave him a quick kiss. "If you don't like playing football, that's reason enough not to sign."

Cal shook his head. "But that's the hell of it. I do like playing soccer. I'm sure I'll always play, coach, help kids learn it. And I have no idea what I would do instead. If I had a plan, I'd go with it, walk away from the contract. But jeez, do I have a right to leave all that money behind, disappoint the team and the investors, for a whim? When I don't even know what I want to do instead?"

Angel slapped the table. "It's your life. You have the right to do anything you want."

Eli felt a moment's panic. If she only knew it was her life too. But he was out of fancy phrases. He got up and walked around the table to Cal. Putting his arms around him, he kissed the man on his neck. "You're a good man, Charlie Brown. You'll figure it out." He turned and started walking to the front door. "I gotta get back to work. See you guys later." And he did walk, though he felt like running.

Chapter Thirteen

Angel slipped out the front door while Cal was lying in the solarium mulling over the contract. It was almost dark. She padded around the house in her soft boots, making little scuffing sounds on the grass, and then stepped onto the stone walkway. She was disappointed. Merde, she would have thought Eli would have been of help to Cal instead of making witty, superficial remarks. It just proved she didn't know him very well, and maybe this was a wake-up call.

When she got to the guesthouse, they already had working lights on. She found Eli up on a ladder, installing a polished wood kitchen cabinet. A young man in camo pants was handing him tools. Even with his back turned and his mane of curly hair pulled tight to his head, Eli's beauty still overwhelmed her. He was one sexy piece of work.

Angel, stop thinking with your pussy.

"Mr. Daniels, may I speak with you?"

Eli spun on the ladder, wobbled, and the young man reached up to balance him. Well, shit, she hadn't been that startling. He looked like a proverbial deer in the headlights.

"Uh, hello, An -- uh, Ms. Silvay."

"When you're at a stopping place, may I talk with you? I'll be outside."

"Uh, sure."

She walked out into the twilight away from the harsh work lights. Most of the workmen stopped at three, so he must be working overtime. Interesting, when he knew that Caleb needed advice. But then, he didn't seem very comfortable in the role of advisor.

She wrapped her jacket more tightly around her shoulders. The nights were full-on cold these days. It wasn't too early to snow. She'd love that. It'd been a while since she'd seen the white stuff.

Scuffing on the grass signaled his arrival. She turned in time to see him looking quite uncomfortable. What the hell? The man was easy as sippin' whiskey most of the time. "You're working late."

He glanced around, but not at her face. "Just wanted to get some progress on the kitchen. I still have the entertainment center to finish, and I want to give it good attention."

"And what about your friend who needs attention?"

"What do you mean?"

"Elijah, Edward, whatever the hell your name is, you know Cal is trying to make a life-changing decision and could use some advice."

"He's got you."

"He needs advice from a man, dammit. Maybe someone who's experienced some of the same discrimination and exclusion he has. I can't do that."

"Fuck, neither can I. What am I supposed to say to him? I don't have press after me, and I don't want it… Oh fuck." He turned his back, arms tightly crossed over his chest.

"Eli, you're treating Cal like you don't care, like he's just somebody you fuck."

He turned sharply. His gold eyes bored into hers, glittering in the ambient light. "I didn't ask to see him again. I didn't think I ever would. He's not my responsibility. Just let me do my job."

Damn. She stepped back. "All right. All right. *Bon.*" She wouldn't cry over something so trivial. After all, despite the best sex of this or any other life, she barely knew the man and had no claims on him. She turned and walked toward the house.

"Angel!" The cry sounded strangled. She turned. He hadn't moved, looked like he couldn't, but one arm was extended to her. He stared. "I'm…I'm sorry."

"I'm sorry too, Eli." She turned again.

"No." His voice stopped her, but she didn't turn around this time. "I mean I'm sorry I said those things. I…I didn't mean them."

That made her turn. "I know you didn't mean them. I'm glad you realized it."

He walked slowly toward her, shaking his head. "I've never done anything like this before."

She wasn't sure what he meant exactly, but she picked the "this" that came first to mind. "None of us have. Hell, you and Cal had hardly been with women, I've certainly never been with two men, and while I understand we have some good role models in my cousin and her men, I don't know much about how polite society conducts a ménage."

He was in front of her now. He raised a hand and twisted it in her hair. She wanted to press against that hand. Better not. He smiled. "Is that what we are?"

"You tell me."

His hand dropped, and he sighed. "Look, I don't do relationships, ever. Not with a woman, not with a man, and certainly not with one of each. I don't know why I haven't run. It has something to do with feeling responsible for the job." She started to answer, and he held up a hand. "I know it's more than that. Both of you are, well…different. Special. But can you not read too much into it if I stay?"

She didn't know whether to slap him or kiss him. Mon dieu, what a commitment-phobe. "I think we can manage that. Cal and I are grown-ups, despite certain evidence to the contrary. But only stay if you want to. If you just want to get your work done and move on, fine. We'll leave you alone. I don't recall it was me or Cal doing the seducing."

He had the grace to grin. "Okay, okay. You're hard to resist."

"So are you, so stay if you want. Maybe we'll see you later." She turned and walked into the French doors, leaving him standing on the terrace.

In the warm dining room, she started shaking. For once in her life, she'd just managed a perfect exit. *Let's hear it for the girl.* Now if she could resist running back out there and begging him to stay.

"You all right?" Cal stood leaning against the big table, and the contract had been gathered into a neat pile. Had he signed it?

"Uh, yeah." She got herself to smile. "Just went out to see if Eli is coming to the house for dinner."

"Is he?" Cal looked anxious, and she knew how he felt.

"Uh, not sure. He's trying to get a lot of work done, plus I think he still wants to go to that apartment and change. You know." She took off her coat, threw it over a chair back at the table, and went into the kitchen to see what she might create to take her mind off beautiful, angel-faced men.

She heard Cal's voice behind her. "He's freaking out, isn't he?"

"A little."

"Yeah. When I first met him, he said relationship rhymed with commitment. We've probably tried to get too close."

She whirled on the big boy. "Well, shit, we didn't exactly drag him into bed." She burst into tears. Oh merde, so much for big-exit girl. Cal was there instantly, pulling her into his arms. God, he felt good. Strong, safe, sexy. She wrapped her arms around his neck and tried to stop crying. "Sorry, got no reason. Hell, neither one of you has any ties to me. Plus I'm just going to go back to Africa, so what difference does it make?"

He nuzzled her, and she giggled. "We'll always have ties, Angel. No matter where you go, a piece of me will be with you."

That was it. She started to sob.

He picked her up and carried her into the great room. It was like flying and crying at the same time. Sitting down on the big couch that had seen a fair amount of action the last few days, he cradled her on his lap and rocked. "It's okay, baby. It's okay."

"But if you'll always be with me, does that mean a part of him will always be with both of us? And oh, Cal, how will I live without you?"

"We'll figure it all out. I promise."

She snuffled and wiped at her eyes. She must look like shit. "Aren't I supposed to be helping you with your decision? Not you comforting me?"

"It all comes around, Angel. I'm not gonna sign shit till I'm sure. That much I know."

Another sniff. "Good." So tired and cozy. She snuggled into his shoulder as he rocked and hummed at her.

A voice came from behind her. "Does this mean I should cook dinner tonight?"

She started and tried to look back over her shoulder, but she didn't have to. Cal's expression was that of a very happy man. She rested her head against the big guy again. "Hi, Eli. Yeah. That would be great."

Chapter Fourteen

Cal leaned back in the dining chair, hands over his stomach. "Who knew you could cook?"

Eli pulled the last of the plates from the table and carried them toward the kitchen. True to his word, he'd made spaghetti. Not gourmet like Angel's meals, but damned good.

"I'm a man of many hidden talents."

Cal smiled. Yeah, and a hell of a lot of other hidden stuff, if he didn't miss his guess. He looked at Angel, who was a little quieter than usual. Not sulky, but just like she was walking on eggshells, being careful what she said. He knew a lot of shit had gone down outside. Eli's being here had been touch and go, he was sure of that. But he was here, and Cal tried to make that enough.

Eli came back in with some dishes of ice cream on a tray. "Nothing fancy. Hope everybody likes Rocky Road. I found it in the freezer."

Angel reached for a bowl. "I'd kill for Rocky Road."

"Hmm. Don't think Ben and Jerry require human sacrifice."

She smiled, and it reached her eyes.

Eli put a bowl in front of Cal and took his seat. The tension wasn't unbearable, but it was there. "Uh, what did you decide about the contract?"

So, he was going to pet the elephant in the room after all. "I've decided not to decide until I'm sure."

"Probably wise." His eyes didn't quite meet Cal's. "What will make you sure?"

"Don't know, but I think I'll know it when I see it."

"Good. Good."

Cal wondered what Eli really wanted to know. Why did the subject make him so nervous?

"Uh, by when do you have to decide?"

Cal tilted back in the chair. "I'm sure they'd like to have it yesterday, but the team doesn't start practice for a few weeks, so I should have time."

Eli took a bite of ice cream. "To look for signs and portents?"

"Something like that."

Eli ate quietly.

Angel finished scraping her bowl. "That was yummy. You know what, you guys, I think maybe I haven't gotten the jet lag out of my system. I'm pretty tired. I think I'll go to bed."

"Want us to tuck you in?" Cal gave her an eyebrow waggle.

"Lovely as that sounds, I may actually be too tired for fucking, uh, I mean tucking." She winked.

Cal got up and put a hand on her head. "You okay, baby?"

"Yeah. Just tired, I think."

"Get in my bed, okay?" He kissed her neck.

She looked up, caressed his face, and smiled. "You couldn't keep me out."

He gave her a gentle kiss on those pink, upturned lips.

Eli came around the table. "Can I have one of those too?"

She gave him a more lingering kiss. A makeup smooch, Cal figured. She smiled, got up, and headed toward the stairs.

"Sleep well." She did look kind of dragged out. She probably wasn't used to as much sex as they'd been having. Hell, who was?

Eli called, "We'll come keep you warm soon." That got a parting grin. He looked at Cal. "Think she's okay?"

"Yeah, it's a long way from Africa, and she's been going full throttle since she got here."

Eli started gathering bowls and silverware. Cal grabbed the rest and followed that tight ass into the kitchen. There were a few plates and glasses stacked on the counter. "I'll put the stuff in the dishwasher."

Cal bent down and opened the dishwasher door, grabbing a few plates and arranging them in the racks. He felt hands caressing his hips.

"Mmmm, I like that pose a lot. Would you like me to take advantage of it?"

Cal closed the dishwasher and rose halfway, putting his hands on the counter. It still left him bent at the waist, ass sticking out, legs wide. "Do you have to ask?"

"Hell no." Cal waited for his sweats to come down. Nothing. He'd raised his head from his arms to glance back when a hand came in front of his face.

"Hold still." The command in Eli's voice snapped him to attention. He froze. A napkin appeared in front of his face. What the hell…? He started to look back. "I said don't move." The napkin covered Cal's eyes, and he felt it tied tightly behind his head. He gasped. Panic or excitement? He wasn't sure of the difference. "Just do as I say. Do you understand?"

Chills skittered up Cal's spine. He'd always been a top. Why did he love this so much? "Yes, yes, I understand."

He strained to hear Eli moving around. It sounded like he left the kitchen for a minute. Then strong, rough-skinned hands pulled up his shirt, grabbed his sweatpants, and yanked them down to his ankles in one motion. Oh man, this was getting better and better. He spread his legs a little more. Crap, he wanted it so bad. He tried to widen his legs, but the sweatpants pulled tight. He started to reach down to pull them away, but Eli grabbed his hand and slapped it back on the counter. "I said don't move, boy."

Cal obeyed instantly. Soft lips caressed his ear. "You want this bad, don't you? You can't wait for this hot cock in your tight ass, can you?"

Cal shook his head. A rough hand in his hair yanked his head back. "Answer me. Tell me how much you want it."

"I want it so bad, Eli. Jesus, I can't wait. Put it in me, please." It was true. Every nerve ending tingled. His butt was on fire just wanting.

"That won't do it, baby. That's not nearly enough to get this cock in you. Let's hear some real begging."

"Please, please put it in me."

"Put what in you?"

"Your cock. Your beautiful cock."

"You think it's beautiful?"

"God, yes. I dream about it. I want it all the time." Shit, it was true. "I want you, Eli. Take me, please. Take me hard, please. I'm begging, please."

One long, hot, hard slide, and his ass was full. It hurt, and yet it felt better than anything in life. "Holy shit!" He hoped his cries didn't wake Angel, but man, there was no help for it. Jesus H.

Eli pounded into him. "You love it, don't you? You love having this pretty, girlie-boy's cock ramming your ass, don't you?" He grabbed Cal's hair, then wrapped his other hand around Cal's throbbing, bobbing cock. With deep, hard pulls, he milked him.

"Yes, yes. Harder, please. Please."

Eli just kept pounding and stroking.

Oh, God. Perfect. So right. He loved this. He'd never known anyone so perfect for him. Had to come. Had to. *Yes.* The heat started down around his knees. Like a molten river of flame, it spread faster and faster up his groin, into his spine, and blazed up into his head and out his cock. He felt like his head came off. "Shit! Baby, baby, I love…" He panicked. *No, can't say that. Stop.* He hauled back those three little letters that would end it all. "This, this, I love this." And he felt his cock spout cum like a fire hose all over the dishwasher door.

"Ahhh." Eli's body froze and then shuddered and bucked as Cal imagined his hot cum filling the condom deep in his ass. Just the idea thrilled him.

Eli fell over Cal's back. A nearly limp hand pulled off the blindfold. "You just do it for me."

As declarations went, it was no romance novel, but he'd take whatever he could get.

"Come on, let's go crawl in with Angel. We can start the dishwasher in the morning."

Yeah, the dripping dishwasher.

They moved pretty slowly, but supporting one another, they managed to get the lights out and climb the stairs. Cal couldn't stop from thinking about what he'd nearly said. Shit, that would have screwed the pooch. *Say "I love you" to Elijah, and I wouldn't be able to look fast enough to see his dust trail as he left.* What a weird trick of fate. He'd finally found not one, but *two* people he could fall in love with, and one hated relationships and the other one lived in Africa. Cosmic joker strikes again.

* * * * *

"Em, Roan, come here," Jake Martin whispered and gestured to his lovers as he peeked though the guest room door. When they came up behind him, he opened the door a little wider. "Look."

Em slipped under his arm, and Roan bent over her head. "Oh my God." She slapped a hand over her mouth. She backed away, taking Roan with her, and Jake shut the door again.

Roan laughed softly. "Well, if we were concerned about his being lonely, this sure puts our worries at ease. Who do you suppose they are?"

Em looked up at the green-eyed beauty. "I can't see the guy very closely, but I think the girl is my cousin.

"Girl?" Jake quietly opened the door again. From the light in the hall, he could just make out his brother, gold-and-brown-streaked hair lying on a pillow, his body wrapped around a young boy. Jake sure as hell hoped that kid was old enough to be in this situation. The boy, in turn, curved around a very pretty blonde girl. He closed the door again. "You never said your cousin was so glamorous."

"Glamorous? Angel? She's pretty enough, but…what do you mean?"

"All those masses of golden curls. Wow."

"Open the door again." Jake complied, and she looked in, then pulled back with a big grin. "Sweetheart, unless I've lost my guydar, those blond curls belong to a man. Angel is definitely the one in the middle."

"But that's a boy…oh."

"You remember me telling you that my cousin looks like a pretty boy." Jake nodded. "That's her."

Roan shook his head. "Son of a bitch, I never knew Caleb liked girls much at all, except as friends, of course."

Jake shrugged. "He told me he'd been with girls back when he was still exploring his sexuality. But I don't think there have been any females for a while."

Em wagged her butt as she turned down the hall toward their bedroom. It made a funny picture with the massive belly swinging the opposite way. "We Silvays just have a way of turning you guys bisexual."

Jake and Roan both laughed. Jake put an arm around each of his lovers. That was certainly the truth.

Chapter Fifteen

Eli slipped quietly out the bedroom door and down the hall. Angel and Cal were still asleep, and he didn't want to wake them, but he did want to get a start on the day. At least he could make some coffee and find some cereal for everyone before he headed to the guesthouse.

Jesus, wasn't he the domestic one? He knew what he was here for, and it wasn't to make coffee.

He stopped and looked out the window in the sitting area. Gorgeous view over gardens, fields, and trees almost bare for winter. Did he know what he was here for? To finish the job he'd started, yes. But what job? The cabinetry? Persuading Cal to sign the contract? Or figuring out what that big guy and cute little tomboy actually meant to him?

They'd given him a perfect out -- finish his job and walk away -- but here he was. Was it self-interest or concern for Angel and her organization? Hell, she was a good person and didn't deserve to be a pawn in his bastard father's schemes. He had to be sure Cal signed. Was that the reason he was still here?

Shit, this was way too much introspection before coffee.

He pulled away from the window and headed downstairs. Halfway down, he smelled the unmistakable aroma of espresso. Yum. WTF? There were no houses nearby. Maybe the guys on the job site got an espresso maker? Not bloody likely.

Quietly he moved through the great room, the dining area, and toward the kitchen. The smell got stronger. He peeked around the corner. At the stove, back turned to Eli, earbuds firmly in place, and tight butt bouncing to some unheard music, was a man. He was wearing slim jeans and a long-sleeved T-shirt that hugged a body Eli could only describe as gorgeous. Tall, lean, broad-shouldered. His shiny, brown-black hair brushed his shoulders.

This must be one of the homeowners. He started to say hi when the man turned. *OMG.* Eli lost his train of thought. He had simply never seen anyone so beautiful. Large, luminous eyes that might be green. A slender nose and lips… Shit, he could create poetry to that mouth. The guy smiled, flashing white. It was too much. Eli sat hard on the bar stool nearest him.

The man came forward, pulling out his earbuds and wiping his hands on a dishtowel. "Hi, I'm Roan."

"You're, uh…"

He smiled again. Same heart-stopping response. "Yes, Roan Black."

"You're, uh…"

He cocked his head, still grinning. Yeah, he'd seen this catatonic response before. "A model, yes."

"Jesus, you are fucking gorgeous."

"Thank you. And for that matter, so are you. Have you ever considered modeling? I know some photographers that would kill for your face."

"Oh shit, no." Eli shook his head to clear it. "Sorry, I'm kind of shy of people in groups."

The gorgeous man, Roan, grinned again. "And you are…?"

"Oh, sorry. Edward, uh, Elijah. Elijah Daniels. Actually, I work for you. I'm the finish carpenter."

"Oh yes." He leaned on the island, and the proximity to his face only increased its beauty. "Bill told me he'd had to change carpenters. I must say, my brother-in-law is taking advantage of the resources available to him out here in the country." Again with the teeth.

Shit. "So, you know…?"

"We got home very late last night and came to check on Cal. So you and Cal and Angel have been lovers since you got here?" His question was matter-of-fact, which Eli figured made sense in light of his own living arrangements.

Still, pretty awkward. He'd hoped to avoid this meeting altogether. Get the job done and be gone. "Actually, Cal and I knew each other before. It was just a coincidence we met again here." Yeah, a manipulated coincidence.

"Interesting. So how is my guesthouse, Mr. Daniels?"

"Please call me Eli. And I don't want you to think I've been shirking the job because of… I really have been working."

The man had the sweetest smile. "I never thought anything else. I just want to know how things are going, and you're here for me to ask. Plus I want you to know that anyone who makes Cal happy is good with me."

Double shit. "Oh, it's not like that…"

A tiny crease appeared between the perfect brows. "You don't make him happy?"

Eli slumped on the bar stool. "Look, sorry, yes, we are lovers. It's just kind of casual, so I didn't want to give the wrong impression."

"I see." Those heavily lashed eyes were green, and they looked like they could see through steel. Eli needed kryptonite to fool this one. "Well, I'm glad you and Cal and Angel have found a happy diversion." He moved back to the stove. "I'm about to make some eggs. Are you hungry?"

Oh, hell no. This man he worked for was not making him breakfast. "Thanks, no. Actually, I came down to get an early start outside. I'd take some of that coffee, though, if you wouldn't mind."

"Sure. I've got some to-go cups down here. We keep them for our drives to town. I'll give you one."

Roan grabbed a plastic insulated thermos from a lower cabinet and started filling it with coffee. "Cream? Sugar?"

"A little cream, thanks. You're up early after driving half the night."

He brought the cup over to Eli. "Jake and I try to give each other some alone time with Em." He smiled. "I woke up early, so I slipped out."

Jesus. Could he take all this domestic love? "Thanks for the coffee. I've got to get to work."

"I'll come out in a while to see the progress."

"Great." Eli tried to walk slowly toward the front door. The guy was so nice and so smart. Chances were the brother and the woman would be too. He couldn't afford to get any more entangled. He felt like a complete fraud in the middle of these good people. And of course, there was Cal…and Angel. Man, he so wanted to believe leaving them wasn't going to hurt like hell. And he also wanted to believe in Santa Claus.

* * * * *

Cal smelled bacon. At least he thought that was what it was. Whoa, monstrously hungry. What time was it? He felt Angel stir beside him. He ran a hand past her body. No Eli. Could he be cooking?

He unwrapped himself from around that little, slim body and rolled to the side of the bed.

"What time is it?" Her voice sounded foggy.

"Don't know. Hang on." He leaned back so he could see the clock on Eli's side of the bed. Whoops. Eli's side. That thought stopped him for a second. "It's almost eight thirty. We really slept in."

She sat up and rubbed a hand over her turned-up nose. "I feel like I just went to bed."

"Nope. You got more than ten hours."

"Do I smell bacon?"

"Yeah, I think maybe Eli is cooking. I'm gonna take a quick shower. Want me to wash your back?"

"Sure. I won't be the most energetic participant, but maybe a good back washing will wake me up." She gave him that sly wink.

He grabbed her for a hug. "Hey, we can save back washing for later. Come on into the shower and…I'll really wash your back."

One thing led to another, and back washing prompted a little…back washing, but the two of them were dry, dressed in sweats, and heading for the smell of food in less than thirty minutes. They tumbled down the steps, and Cal thought the angel looked for all the world like a puppy heading for a treat. They rounded the corner, and both stopped.

"Em!" Angel squealed, ran, and hurled herself at the seated woman, despite the obvious nine-month barrier in her lap. Em stretched out her arms and managed to get most of the slender body into an embrace.

"Angel. Oh my gosh, it's been so long. How are you? Let me look at you." She held her away, examining the tomboy body and pretty face like a scientist looking at a favorite specimen. "You look a little tired, sweetie, but otherwise marvelous. Sweetheart, this is Jake, and the ugly one is Roan."

She got hugs from the two men and looked appropriately awed at the beauty so amply displayed. "Jesus, Em. Is there a factory where they make these gorgeous guys?"

Em chuckled. "You ought to know."

Angel smiled at Cal, who hung back a little to give the cousins space.

Em scooted with some effort back onto the stool. "Africa hasn't been treating you badly, I think."

"Oh no, cuz, I love it. The people are great, the work is challenging, and the need is enormous. Right up my alley."

Cal looked at the little critter. God, he respected her so much. Here was a person who made a difference. Like Em and Jake, and even like Roan the supermodel, who used big chunks of his considerable fortune to build and subsidize low-income housing. They were incredible people, and somehow blocking a ball didn't quite measure up. Of course, there were balls and there were balls. He grinned.

"Hey there, big guy. What're you grinning at?" Jake hopped off another bar stool and came over to give his brother a hug. The handsome blond looked up at Cal through his mild-mannered-reporter wire rims. "You've just been getting in all kinds of trouble since we left you, I gather."

Cal tried to look embarrassed. "Yeah." Then he gave his big brother a grin. "But having a hell of a lot of fun."

Angel went into the kitchen to help Roan finish breakfast, and Cal joined Jake in a little table-setting action. When they were finally all seated around the table, Angel seemed to realize she hadn't asked the obvious question. "So aren't you guys home early? How come the late-night arrival? Are you feeling okay?"

Jake gestured with a piece of buttered scone toward Em's belly. "Em was getting a lot of Braxton Hicks contractions. We just thought being closer to home would be better."

Em stopped chewing. "But they stopped, so another false alarm. I'm fine now." She turned to Angel. "I'm really glad you're here, so we can plan."

Jake smiled. "Ah, I see hours of chick time -- planning a birth, the baby's room, the name."

Cal laughed. "Us guys can watch sports."

Roan leaned over and patted Em's belly. "Sorry. I'm the gay one. Count me in on the chick time." He sipped some coffee. "Although I have to go into the city tomorrow for a shoot. When I knew we were coming home, I accepted it. Don't do too much fun stuff without me, okay?"

Em leaned over and kissed those pouty lips. "We won't leave you out, my love. But be careful. They say maybe snow tomorrow."

Jake started clearing some dishes. "Actually I need to go in to the computer lab tomorrow. They're suffering from the lack of their fearless leader." He winked at Em. "I'm a poor substitute, but I need to do my best." He threw a hand to his head in mock suffering.

"You'll get me on the phone or a video chat if you need me, right?"

Jake came around and patted Em's belly. "Yes, both of you."

Roan looked at Cal, then pointedly at Angel. "So who wants to tell us about Mr. Beautiful, who's slaving away in our guesthouse? When he's not slaving in your bed, that is, Mr. Martin."

Cal could feel himself blushing. "Well, I met him in a bar." He nodded at his brother. "You know, Jake, the Flamingo. And we, uh, hooked up, but, uh, well, I never thought I'd see him again. Then a few days later, I come back from a trip to the city and find him sitting at the dining room table having tea with Angel."

Angel took up the thread. "See, Cal had asked me to check in with the carpentry guy when he came on the job to make sure he knew who he could go to with questions. And, well, I recognized his obvious charms but had no idea he knew Cal."

Em interrupted. "Wait, you mean he didn't come here looking for Cal? You sure he wasn't just faking it?"

Cal shook his head. "No, uh, we didn't even exchange last names or anything."

"He could have seen you play on TV."

"No, I don't think he knew much about the soccer till he got here. It was a coincidence."

"Jeez, some coincidence." Em didn't seem convinced.

"Yeah, well, he seemed to think it was pretty weird too."

Roan smiled. "I guess the real question is whether you two are attached to the guy."

Angel frowned. "Unfortunately he's pretty much a reclusive commitment-phobe. Yeah, I like him a lot. I think Cal does too. But we're probably better off not getting our hopes up. I think he's a bad bet long-term."

Shit. The truth hurt. Cal felt like someone had stabbed him in the gut. He looked up in time to see Jake staring at him.

Roan, the romantic, didn't give up. "Well, Cal should still go down and invite him to join us all for dinner so we can put our stamp of approval on him." He laughed. "Actually I just want to look at him again. Wait till you get a load of this guy, Em. He's got a face like a Botticelli angel and a body like a young Greek god."

Em reached over and took her lover's hand. "Look who's talking."

Cal stood and started clearing dishes. "I'll do it, but I'll wait until later in the day. Eli's pretty intent on the work, so I'll let him get more finished before I interrupt him." He wasn't sure if Eli would come to dinner. This was a lot of family for a commitment-phobe.

Chapter Sixteen

Cal walked out the French doors and down toward the guesthouse. Twilight colored the sky, but it was cold, and he shivered. Roan and Angel were having a ball playing gourmet cooks in the kitchen, although Angel didn't quite seem her spunky self. Em and Jake were snuggling on the couch and trying out baby names.

Cal loved the family feel of it, even if it was a pretty unconventional family. He and Jake came from the best of families. His mom and dad had never expected their kids to be any particular way. They adored Roan and worshipped Em. The fact that their middle son lived with two people in a ménage was fine with them. Happiness was the criteria. Jeez, they'd probably love Angel. Maybe Eli too. Cal sighed. *Get over it. Not gonna happen.*

As he neared the guesthouse, he saw Eli standing outside with his phone to his ear. He was gesturing angrily. Cal stopped at the sound of his raised voice. "How the hell would I know? I don't make his decisions. Give me a fucking break, will you? I can't control the situation. No, I don't want that. No. Fuck!" He looked up and saw Cal. His face registered panic. What the hell was going on? Eli pulled the phone from his ear, faced Cal head-on, and screamed, "Are you going to sign that fucking contract, yes or no? Just make up your fucking mind!"

Cal froze. What the shit difference did it make to Eli whether he signed that contract or not? And who the hell was he talking to? "Who wants to know?"

Eli put the phone back up to his ear. He listened for a moment and extended the phone to Cal. The look on his face was pure pain.

Ice. Straight up Cal's spine. Betrayal. Loss.

Cal could barely hear Eli's voice. "I'm sorry."

Cal took the phone. "Who is this?"

"You already know the answer, don't you, Cal?"

That snaky, nasal voice was unmistakable. "So what the hell is this about? Why are you talking to Eli?" But Cal was afraid he already knew. Suddenly the golden hair and the pale eyes made sense.

"The man standing next to you is, of course, my son. And you already know what this is about. I am currently in the dining room of an inn a couple of miles from your brother's house. Elijah will bring you here. I expect to see you in about ten minutes."

"Why should I come see you when you've obviously been spying on me and trying to manipulate me?"

"Ah, that is the question, isn't it? Let's just say the futures of two people you care about are at stake. And, of course, your own. Everyone who knows you says you're a good man, Caleb. So I imagine I'll be seeing you soon." The line went dead.

Cal's arm dropped. The phone slipped from his fingers onto the damp grass. He'd thought he'd protected himself from the disappointment he knew was coming from Eli, but this? Not on the radar. And the protection? A pipe dream. No amount of telling himself that he couldn't have Eli for keeps had worked. Somewhere deep in his heart, he still had hoped. Not anymore. "So you knew about this?"

Eli's face said it all.

"Take me to him."

Eli didn't move for a second, just stared down at the ground. Then he leaned down and picked up the phone, slipping it into his pocket. "I didn't know at first." He looked up, and a little light from the work site glinted off his golden eyes. "I didn't know when I came here that he was using me. I actually thought he'd done something nice for a change. Then I saw you and realized the coincidence was too much to believe. He has me followed."

Cal gazed back at that beautiful face. Shit, beautiful *lying* face. "But you could have told me. His *son*, for Christ's sake. You lied day after day. You let him use you in ways I don't even understand."

Eli sighed. Some resignation there, not that Cal thought Eli gave a shit if he'd hurt him, hurt Angel. "Yeah, well I don't understand them completely either. But believe me, it gets worse. Follow me in your car; then I can just go on."

"So you're leaving? You've done your job, and you're gone?"

The angelic face looked full-on pissed. "If I had finished my fucking job, I wouldn't be here now. My job, as you call it, is to do these cabinets." He pointed back to the guesthouse. "Otherwise I would have been on a fucking ride to Timbuktu again, trying to escape my fucking father. I have one more day's work, I figure, and then I'm outta here." He turned and stalked toward the front of the house, where he kept the bike.

Cal stared after him. Did the guy think he'd just get to finish the guesthouse like nothing had occurred? But he didn't want to tell Jake and Roan and Em what was happening yet. And he couldn't make Roan get another carpenter this close to the end of the job. Shit, he'd just grit his teeth and hope his heart didn't bleed all over the fucking rugs.

Cal went up to the house and told them he'd be late for dinner and that Eli wasn't coming. When Jake tried to get details, Cal just told him he was in a hurry and he'd explain later. Now, in his car, following Eli on his bike kicked Cal in the gut. Wave after wave of memory swept over him from their first night together, when Eli had followed Cal to the motel. The passion, the surrender, the amazing intensity he'd never had with any other person, man or woman, although Angel came close. Yeah, and he remembered the cold sheets and cold pit in his stomach the next morning when the bastard had left. Shit, he wasn't looking forward to this meeting, but maybe he was better off without Eli. Crap, Elias Dante's son.

The inn was old Connecticut money -- quiet, elegant, and restrained. Dante probably figured it would discourage drama. Cal and Eli followed the maître d' through a room with crystal glassware and linen tablecloths to a secluded booth by the back wall. Both Cal and Eli were very casual for a place that obviously had a dress code.

Hell, Eli was in work clothes. But no one stopped them after Eli dropped the Dante name.

Elias Dante stood as they approached. Cal was struck again by the resemblance, although Eli's face was feminine beautiful, despite its structure, while Elias's face was more angular, harder, tougher.

"Good to see you, Son. Cal." He nodded. "Thank you, Winston." He smiled at the maître d'. "Will you have someone bring us some more mineral water when you have a chance?" Oh shit, the guy was a snake charmer.

Eli slid into the booth closer to his father, leaving Cal on the end.

Dante gestured to the table, the charming host. "What can I get you both to eat or drink?"

Cal leaned on the table and clasped his hands to keep from hitting someone. "I have dinner waiting with my *family*. Just get to the point, Dante."

The expression on that handsome face shifted just slightly, but Cal knew it was dangerous. "As you say. I've told you that we very much want you on the Rocket Dogs next year, Cal. In fact, we want you to start as goalie." Cal started to protest, and Dante held up his hands. "That is open to negotiation. But whether or not you play is *not* open to negotiation. I am old enough to be your father, Cal, and as a father of a son" -- he pointed idly to Eli -- "I know that sometimes I must step in and decide what is in a young man's best interest."

The fucking, arrogant bastard.

Dante continued his fairy tale. "I'm sure you'll agree that the contract we sent you is more than fair for a young man not yet fully tried."

"Yes, I do agree, but --"

Again the graceful hand. "You see, I feel an obligation to keep you from throwing that all away, as my son has done."

Cal couldn't take the self-righteous monologue another second. Trying to keep his voice down, which made him even madder, he spit between his teeth. "You don't give a shit about me."

"Of course I do." He gave a tight smile. "You're not only talented, you're big and handsome and will pull female fans to the team in droves, which represents a lot of money at the gate and in advertising, now, doesn't it?"

"And you're just going to overlook the inconvenient fact that I'm gay?"

He smiled again. "Well now, you're not really gay, are you, since the person you are currently shacking up with happens to be a woman."

Cal looked hard at Eli. Eli shook his head. "I didn't tell him."

The SOB. "So you're having me watched?"

Dante chuckled and brushed it aside. "Oh, I watch everything I value."

"Spy, you mean?"

The smile vanished. "Semantics."

"I also happen to be" -- Cal glanced at Eli -- "until very recently, *shacking up* with your son. And the press has already started to get wind of the fact that I like boys, so you're going to have to deal with it very soon. What's that going to do to your advertising revenue?"

Dante shook his head as if indulging a child. "Simple. You'll appear in public with your little girlfriend." As Cal tried to interject, he rushed on. "And if she is going back to Africa, which may not occur, of course, then we'll simply find you another girlfriend. I'll threaten those smarmy tabloids with lawsuits for defaming our upstanding young player, and as long as you don't come out, the press will have to play along. They do it every day in every sport. They don't really want to believe their superstars are homosexual, and they don't want to get sued."

Cal took a deep breath. Okay, here was the scary question. "And if I don't want to stay in the closet for five years? If I don't want to kick a ball around for my whole youth when I might be doing something really useful with my life?”

“Oh Cal, Cal. I’m sure you recognize that I’m a man who gets what he wants. I try to do that by giving other people what they want. My son, for example.” He smiled beatifically at Eli. “He wants to live a quiet life out of the public spotlight. He wants to do his little woodcrafting things and pick up pretty boys in bars without interference and without his customers and the parents of the children he teaches knowing he’s gay. Also, without the press knowing who he is and where he is. He has been fairly successful in achieving what he wants…because I help him. Because I watch to be sure the press don’t find him. Because I cross the palms of those that do find him with silver so that he can remain anonymous.”

Cal glanced between Elias and Elijah. It must be true, because Eli wasn’t defending himself. Just staring at his hands.

Cal snorted. “And you do this out of the goodness of your heart? Shit, I doubt it. You probably don’t want the press focusing on the fact that Elias Dante has a gay son.”

“Regardless of my motivations, know with certainty that I can and will remove my oversight of Eli’s life and let the hounds descend. In fact, I will even be the pointer dog who shows them the way.”

Cal glanced at Eli. The face was set. The man wasn’t going to show his father he cared, but Cal knew him well enough to know he cared a lot. Shit, Cal wanted to hit him…and hold him. “And this concerns me how?”

“Well, Cal, I think you do care, but regardless, my story is not concluded. I believe that your little girlfriend works for Global Outreach? And what she wants is to continue doing so?”

Cold chills raised goose bumps on his arms. “Yes.”

“Perhaps you aren’t aware that I am one of the principal contributors to Global Outreach. And, while it would benefit me a great deal if this young lady did *not* return to Africa, I will remain one of the organization's principal contributors right after you sign the contract. Your girlfriend need never know that she is returning to Africa out of the goodness of *my* heart."

"You bastard."

"Yes, well, as you say, although my parentage is well documented." He grinned at his own joke. "There are many charities in the world, Cal. I will simply choose to shift my loyalty to a different one. And of course, there are others who will follow my lead."

Eli finally spoke. "Jesus, Elias. I honestly never knew you were such a bastard. I thought you just liked torturing me."

"Ah, Eli, just consider it a lesson in how to live life in the fast lane, which you will be joining. I assure you, if Mr. Martin doesn't make the right decision, you will have little choice but to come and work for me." He reached behind him and took a menu that he must have set aside before they got there. "Now, I'm hungry, and I want to eat. If you both want to join me, you're welcome. Otherwise, Caleb, I'll expect that contract on my desk... Hmm. Let's see, tomorrow is Friday. Shall we say, Monday morning? No, Tuesday. I'll schedule a press conference to announce your decision. My assistant will call with the details. Good to see you both." He gestured to the waiter and looked down at his menu. They were dismissed.

Outside, Cal wrapped his peacoat around him against the cold. Man, the temperature was dropping, and it felt like snow. Shit, the weather was warmer than he felt. He headed toward his car.

"Cal."

He turned and saw Eli a few steps behind him. Still beautiful. The snake.

"When you're making your decision, don't consider my situation. It's all about Angel. Global Outreach sounds like a good organization that deserves to exist. Just think of that, not me."

"I wasn't planning to."

"If that's true, good. I'll just run again and try to find a place to hide where he can't find me for a while. I've done it before and succeeded for a few months. You're right. He really doesn't want the press to latch on to the fact that the scion of the Dante clan is a flaming homo, so maybe he won't want to follow through with his threats. You and Angel figure out what to do. I'll finish up my work tomorrow. Then I'm outie."

"I thought you loved your home in Vermont."

"Nah. I never get too attached."

"Yeah. I know." Cal stared at Eli. Man, it was work not loving him. "Why didn't you tell us, Eli? Maybe we could have figured something out. Why did you keep it a secret? Why did you try to manipulate me for him when you could have just told me?" His voice broke. Shit. *Wimp!*

Eli stared at his boots and shook his head. "I didn't want you to know I was his son and that he controlled my life. At first, I thought there was a possibility you might actually want to sign the contract. Hell, not many people would give up that kind of chance. When I knew you didn't, I was in even deeper. You and Angel are so capable, so independent. How could I tell you I'm nothing but a leech? That I only get to live my life because my father lets me. I'm so proud of not taking his money. Shit, I should have taken it and used it against him. But I didn't have the balls. I'm sorry."

"So am I." Cal walked back to his car.

Chapter Seventeen

Merde. Where the hell was he? Angel tried not to appear anxious. She didn't want to worry Jake and the others, but shit, something was up. Cal had looked stressed when he came in earlier, and Eli had to be involved. *Don't assume. Don't assume.*

They'd eaten, saving a plate for Cal, and now they were all trying to appear relaxed, watching television. Angel knew everyone had half a mind on the missing brother. When the front door opened, Em let out a breath. "Finally!"

They didn't all jump up, but everyone stared toward the entry. Very subtle. She heard the hall closet open and close as Cal put away his coat, and then he walked in. Oh yeah, world on his shoulders.

Roan got up. "Hi, Cal. Sit down; I'll get you some food."

"Thanks, Roan. I appreciate you saving something for me."

Angel tried to lighten the mood. "It was a close thing. Roan made turkey meat loaf, and we had to rescue the last piece from your ravening brother."

Cal smiled, but there wasn't much heart in it. He sat on the couch next to her and took her hand. Oh my God, he was the sweetest man. Mon grand. Mon cher.Mon *belle* grand. How could she leave him?

Jake turned off the TV. "Come on, bro, what's up?"

Roan's voice came from the kitchen. "Hang on. I want to hear too." A couple of seconds later, he walked in with a heaping plate of meat loaf, mashed potatoes, brussels sprouts à la Roan, and a glass of beer. Comfort food of the best kind. He set it down on the coffee table in front of Cal. "If you need to switch to whiskey, just let me know."

"Thanks. This looks fantastic." He took a bite of meat loaf and shut his eyes appreciatively. Angel knew he wasn't just being polite. Roan's cooking was good enough to penetrate even the most depressed mood.

Em interrupted their tense waiting. "So eat, enjoy. What do you think of the name Arianne? Arianne Martin-Black?"

Cal managed a grin. "Isn't that a little effeminate for my nephew?"

"If it's a girl, silly. For a boy, how about Andres, you know, like the Spanish? Or maybe Elias…"

"No!" Cal actually rose up out of his seat a little.

That shut up the group.

He sat back hard. "Sorry. Not my favorite name right now."

Jake looked serious. "Okay, you better tell us."

Cal wiped his mouth with a napkin. "You know that grand coincidence none of us believed? Eli showing up here by accident?"

Jake frowned. "Not a coincidence, right?"

"Right. Eli is the fucking son of the fucking financier who's trying to get me to sign the Rocket Dogs contract."

"Oh no." Angel slapped a hand over her mouth. Merde. Bile rose in her throat, burning and bitter. She now knew what getting kicked in the stomach felt like.

Cal reached over and took her hand and pulled her closer. "Sorry, sweetheart. His father put him here to manipulate me into signing the contract. He swears he didn't know at the beginning, but when he found out his father had put him here on purpose, he didn't say anything. He just kept lying." He kissed her nose, then looked up at the family. "In his defense, I guess, I should tell you that Dante holds the key to Eli's way of life. He values his freedom and privacy over everything, and his father is threatening to out him and sic the press on him if I don't comply."

Jake sat back in his chair, frowning. "It doesn't sound to me like you owe the man anything."

"No. I told him that, and he agreed."

The tears pushed at her eyes again. "He could have told us. Maybe we could have helped him." She felt exhausted. Every muscle ached. She leaned back against the comfy couch. Cal slipped his arm around her and pulled her against him. Warm, safe. But the loss of Eli felt like a wound in her heart.

She heard Cal's voice get softer, but it rumbled. "That wasn't Dante's only threat, I'm afraid. He got much worse."

Em's voice. "What else, Cal?"

She felt lips against her hair. "Dante is a big contributor to Global Outreach. Remember, you told me, Angel?"

She pulled away and looked up at him, nodding. *Oh no. No.* "You mean…? How does he know you'd care?" She was sitting up straight now. "What the hell? Why would he…? You mean he's going to…?" She knew she was sputtering, but how could someone be so cruel?

"He said he'd withdraw his support of Global Outreach unless I sign. He said others would go with him. Angel, I'm so sorry. This is all my damned fault."

She shook her head helplessly. "Not your fault."

Jake exploded. "The bastard. Did Eli tell him about Angel? Is that how he knows?"

A knife twisted in her heart.

"Eli swears not. Apparently, Dante has his spies. He probably has photos of the three of us. It's pretty creepy to realize just how thoroughly this guy 'watches what he values,' as he says."

Too much. Tears started running down her face. "This man is using me against you. I hate this. It's so evil." She sobbed, and Cal pulled her tight. Oh dieu, she'd lived her life so independently. She loved her family, but she'd never asked anyone for anything. Now her world was a mass of ties and complications. Every one of them broke her heart.

Cal rocked her. "Don't worry, Angel. I'm going to sign. I can't let the man destroy the lives of a lot of good people just because I can't make a decision about my future."

Em sighed. "Cal, you can't let him win."

"No, it's okay, Em. Hell, most people would kill to have the kind of opportunity this guy is forcing on me. I admit, I hate that he gets away with manipulating people's lives, but I guess when you have that much money, you can do anything. I'll sign for five years, and then we'll see what's next."

Jake jumped up from his chair and started pacing. "Hell, Cal, you know what'll be next. He'll demand five more years if you're making him money. And if you're injured or lose your edge, you'll be so indebted to agents and assistants and publicists, you'll go become a coach or a commentator or something just to keep them paid. Shit, this is your moment. It's the turning point. This decision isn't easy to reverse."

Roan walked up to Jake and put his arms around his lover's waist, leaning his head against his shoulder. "He's right, Cal. Though I'm in a very different industry, I know it's true. So don't decide yet. You have a few days. Let's talk some more. Meanwhile, I think I should fire your beautiful carpenter."

Cal shook his head vehemently. "No, Roan, it's almost done. One more day, he says. You'd never find someone else at this late date. Just let him finish. He'll be gone soon enough."

"You sure? I'm happy to fire his ass."

Cal nodded. "I'm sure. You need to get it done before the weather sets in." He looked like a whipped dog that had been kicked one too many times.

Roan shook his head once. Angel felt like she'd throw up.

Cal looked stricken. She knew he wanted all this drama behind him, even if it meant making the wrong decision. But Global Outreach? It was such a good organization. It helped so many people with very little overhead or administrative expenses. These were the good guys. They couldn't be the loser in her relationship problems. Crap, she felt like someone had drained the life from her.

Merde.

* * * * *

Cal wandered down the hall from his room. He'd just tucked Angel into bed. Poor critter, she was whipped, and this last bombshell had been the finishing touch. Actually, though, she felt feverish. He thought there was more going on than just exhaustion. She'd asked him to give her some homeopathic medicine she kept in her midwife's bag, and he'd also rubbed a little good-smelling Chinese salve on her back. She'd muttered something about the copilot on the flight she'd taken having the flu. Just what she needed. Oh well, she could play baby decorating with Em when she felt better.

He'd lain down with her until she was breathing deeply, but he couldn't sleep. Too restless and confused. A part of him wanted to sign the bloody contract and send it over to Dante. Roan told him not to, and Cal figured he'd trust his brother-in-law with his life, so he'd wait. Of course, it was *his* life they were talking about. Shit, he hated waiting. Maybe another beer or a glass of wine would help put him out. He didn't drink much, so a little went a long way.

He got to the upstairs sitting area when he heard a noise. Was that a moan? For a second, he thought of Angel, but no, it was not that kind of moan.

"Oh, Jake, fuck me, do it harder. God, more."

Cal stopped dead. The door to the master bedroom was slightly ajar. He smiled. This must be the famous dirty talk Jake had confessed about his beautiful lover.

"Give me more. Ram that beautiful cock in me. I love it so much. I love you so much."

His mind conjured the scene, and he shook his head, trying to escape it. Roan with that unparalleled ass in the air, and Jake ramming that cock into it harder and harder, going nuts with his lover's dirty talk. Where was Em? Sleeping or watching the two men, like Angel liked to do?

And suddenly it wasn't Jake, Roan, and Em making love, it was him and Angel and, damn him, the beautiful Eli. *Oh shit*. He grabbed his cock through his sweats and ran back to his room. Crap! Inside the door, he pulled the drawstring loose and ripped his cock out. He went to work on it with both hands. Needed the lube. Still jerking, he stumbled across to the bedside table, let go one hand, and grabbed the bottle. He coated both palms, fell on the bed, and began to stroke. Yeah, one hand up, around the head and down. Other hand up, around the head and down. Jesus, it was Angel's mouth on his cock, sucking him deep into her throat. Deeper and deeper. His hands moved faster. Now it was Eli, stroking him with those rough carpenter's hands while he hammered his dick into Cal's hole. Deeper and harder. Again and again.

How would he ever have this again? He loved Angel, and he hated to admit it, but he loved Eli. The two of them had unlocked some deep and fundamental part of him that no one else had ever touched. They made him vulnerable, and even though he should hate it, he didn't. He loved being open and real. What would happen to that now? Would that part of him go back into hiding? Would he hide more than just being gay? God, Eli. Elijah. His hands pumped frantically. How could he stand to lose him? He pumped faster and faster as heat rolled through his balls and out his rod. Cum spouted from his dick. Yeah, maybe it was melodramatic at twenty-two to say you'd never feel this way again, but he knew it was true. This was a turning point for him. He had a chance to live a real life. If he walked away, everything would always be less.

He lay still, hands on his softening cock, staring into space. His own indecision threatened not just himself, but hundreds, probably thousands of people who relied on the money Dante would withdraw from Global Outreach. And Angel would lose her job, maybe in disgrace. It was so simple to fix it. Just a couple of words written on some paper. But not simple at all, because if he signed, he'd assure that Dante continued to control not only Eli, but Angel and Cal as well. And for how long? Maybe forever.

Shit, there was no good solution. There would be no other time quite like now. No way to undo completely what would be done when he signed that paper. He wiped his hands over his face. Cum and tears. They sure as hell went together.

142

Chapter Eighteen

Even though he felt like somebody had beaten him with a stick, Cal ferried soft-boiled eggs and hot tea up the stairs toward his bedroom. Emotional exhaustion was worse than fifty soccer games.

Angel had the flu, though she was sitting up, trying to be cheerful about it. The house was quiet. Earlier Cal had watched Jake and Roan leave in Roan's big town car, complete with chauffeur. They would drop Jake at his company on Roan's way into the city for his photo shoot. Em was sleeping in this morning, and he hadn't heard a peep from her. He smirked. The randy boys must have worn her out.

Cal looked through the window outside the bedrooms. Man, it looked cold out there, and the sky hung dark, low, and heavy with clouds, but still no snow. On one of his five previous glances out the window, he'd caught a glimpse of Eli moving around inside the building, but no sign now. The guesthouse was nearly complete. Yeah, and Eli was nearly gone.

How did he feel about that? Like he ought to hate the bastard. Why couldn't he do it? Was he some kind of fucking masochist, clinging to a cheating, treacherous SOB who didn't give a shit about him or Angel? No, that wasn't fair. Eli had clearly cared about Angel's organization. Cal sighed.

Crap, the eggs were getting cold. He headed to the bedroom, tapped lightly, and went in. She was curled under the covers in a small ball. "Hey, critter, how're you feeling?"

"Like I want to go back and smack that copilot who probably gave this to me."

"I brought you some breakfast. Think you can get it down?"

"Sure. Let me at it, coach." She sat up, tucked covers around her to keep warm, and accepted the small tray he lowered onto her lap. She tasted the eggs and seemed to like them, because she spooned some more in. He straightened the homeopathic pills and tinctures on her bedside table. Actually, his bedside table, since this was his room, but he'd probably give it over to her tonight. He didn't need the flu.

"Cal…" He looked at her, her short brown hair mussed from the pillow, pink nose and no makeup. She looked even more like a pretty little boy huddled in the big bed. She sipped tea, clearly reluctant to spit the words out. "What are we going to do?"

He sat on the edge of the bed and began massaging her legs through the covers. "I don't know for sure. I'm inclined to think I should just sign the contract. Hell, maybe I'll love it. I mean, I really like playing soccer."

She practically spilled the tea. "Merde, *non*. No one has the right to force you into a life you don't want just because they have money. There is another way. There's a choice. Shakti taught me there's always a choice. We just have to find it. See it clearly."

"Yeah, Roan told me not to decide anything for sure until he comes home tomorrow, so I'll take him at his word."

She sipped again, licking a little spilled tea from her hand. "Actually I meant what are we going to do about Eli? Are we just going to let him walk away?"

"What else can we do? The bastard was using us, Angel, just to get his father off his back. He didn't care about us at all."

"You don't really believe that."

"What should I believe?"

"Cal, if he was really only doing his father's bidding, he would have tried much harder to persuade you to sign. He didn't."

He crossed his arms on his chest. "Yeah, well, he didn't try to talk me out of it either."

"No, but that would have been directly opposed to his own best interest." She looked down. "And mine."

"Yes, but he should have told us, Angel." It came out of his mouth as a wail.

She nodded. "Yes, I know."

"And now he's going, and we don't have any choice in the matter."

She blew her nose. Then smiled a little blearily. "Shakti…"

"Ah yes, I get it. We have a choice. But what do you think that might be?"

"How did you leave it with him?" She set the tea aside and pulled the covers higher.

"You cold?"

"I just have some fever. I think it's probably pretty warm in here."

He tucked the blankets around her neck and shoulders. "Not well." He glanced at her. "I mean, that's how we left it. He said he was leaving as soon as he got the guesthouse cabinetry done. He figured that was a day, so I guess he'll leave tonight or tomorrow morning. He did tell me not to take his father's threats with regard to him into consideration. He said he's run from his father before, and he's willing to do it again. That it shouldn't affect my decision. He said I should only think about you…and me."

"What did you say?"

"That I didn't plan on considering him."

"But that's not true, is it?"

Cal looked down at his hands. "Well, mostly. The main consideration is you, and all the people who will be hurt if Global Outreach is crippled by his withdrawn support."

"It's a good organization. It deserves to exist. I can't believe one man can bring it down."

"He's got big money and huge clout. I have to take the threat seriously."

"Tell me something. What will you do instead of play soccer?"

He loved that she assumed his doing something besides sports was a done deal. "Honestly if I knew that, I'd have left before this. I just keep thinking there's something out there for me, but maybe the fact that I can't find it is a sign." He glanced up. "You know, that I should keep playing soccer."

"Bullshit."

He laughed. "Don't hold back. Tell me how you really feel."

He was joking, but she took him seriously. "I feel that you have great potential to make an impact in this world. Few people feel a deep calling to help others. You simply cannot ignore that."

He ran his hands through the overlong hair he knew was sticking out straight from his head. "I could make a lot of money playing soccer and then use it globally."

She looked into his eyes. It felt more like into his soul. "Is that what you want?"

He shook his head. "No. I want to start today, and I want to help directly. I just don't know how. How did you decide?"

She pulled the cover tighter. "I knew from an early age that I wanted to be in health care. I started to study medicine, but hated the drug-for-every-symptom structure of it. But I noticed that I was drawn to pediatrics and obstetrics. In the hospital, I met a midwife. The rest is history. She was the one who told me about Global Outreach. She had a big family, a bunch of kids, so she couldn't go, but she loved the idea a lot. After I finished my midwife training, I went in, signed up, and never looked back."

"It was that clear."

"Oui. And there's so much more to do. There are people who suffer, like gay men and women with AIDS. They have almost no access to health care. I wish I could do more. But I'm happy helping my moms. Those moms are my family. Those kids are my kids. It was meant to be."

"And what about kids of your own? Your own family?" His heart was beating fast.

She gazed at him, snuffling a bit. "Cal, I think I'm falling in love with you. If I haven't already. I would love to have you in my life. Be a family. Maybe even have one. But first and foremost, I don't think committing yourself to a heterosexual relationship is realistic. You've lived your life as a gay man. That's your identity. You're not attracted to women, as you've told me."

"Obviously you're an exception."

"And I'm honored. But at best, I think we might stay together a year before the pressure of your attraction got the better of us. I would swear to be understanding, but I know it would only stretch so far."

He started to speak, but she interrupted. "There's more to this story. I said I would love to have you in my life. The critical word is 'my.' I don't know if I could bear to choose between you and my work even if there were no other obstacles. I know I couldn't be a soccer wife any more than I could be a soccer mom. It's not in me, Cal. I was born to serve. I can't change that."

He was quiet for seconds. "And if I tell you I think I'm in love with you too?"

He watched tears well up in her eyes and begin to roll down her cheeks onto the pillow. "Then I would say I was thrilled…and that we are the unluckiest of people, and my heart is broken."

Those tears were acid falling on his heart.

He left her there sound asleep a few minutes later. He stood in the hall, back pressed to the door. Shit, she saw things clearly. Was he ready to marry a woman, live a heterosexual life, never have sex with a man again? His heart could imagine it. His cock? Not so much. He pictured Jake, Roan, and Em, the two men passionate lovers but still completed by their woman. It wasn't your usual domestic arrangement, but shit, it worked, and he could clearly see how.

But even if he and Angel could have such a life, it still wouldn't work. She was going back to Africa. That was that. Yeah, and Eli was going somewhere else. He couldn't ask her not to go. He wouldn't ask Eli.

Slipping out of the bedroom, he went back to the window. Staring time. Wow. While he'd been with Angel, the snow had started in earnest. It fell like a white curtain from the sky, so thick he could barely see the guesthouse. He was vaguely aware it was beautiful, but mostly it blocked his view of…who? The man he wanted to see? The man who had lied to him, betrayed him? The man…he loved?

Crap. He leaned his forehead against the cold window glass. That's an idea he'd like to tear from his brain with fingernails. He sighed. Here he stood, a man in love with two people, and he couldn't have either one.

"Cal."

He looked up from the window. Was that Angel? No. Too far. He walked toward the master bedroom door. It was midmorning, and he still hadn't seen Em. "Em, did you call me?"

"Yes, c'mon in."

He opened the door slowly. Holy crap! In the middle of one of the grand Asian carpets, Em, dressed in some soft pajama-looking bottoms and a floppy top, sat on a big blue exercise ball, legs spread to accommodate her huge belly, and slowly rotating her hips. "Hi."

He grinned. "Hi, sis. Did you decide you desperately needed a workout?"

She smiled, he'd have to say radiantly. "No, but the baby did. I'm in labor."

"What? Holy shit!"

She just kept rotating, pausing every few seconds to grimace and breathe with a bit more focus. Hell, he didn't know about the ball thing, but he'd seen enough movies to know about the breathing.

"So am I correct that my cousin is sick as a proverbial hound?"

"Yes, afraid so. I just took her some eggs, and she's sound asleep."

"And my beloveds are at work?"

"Yes, but I'll call them, okay?" He grabbed frantically for his cell, only to discover it wasn't in his pocket. "Damn. It's on my dresser. I'll go get it." He started to run from the room.

"Cal." Again with the breathing. Oh shit, those pains didn't seem very far apart for somebody just starting labor. Wasn't it supposed to take a long time? When the breathing stopped, she tried again. "Calling them will be great. Do that. But, baby, I can see out my window. The expressway is going to be a nightmare. I want them to be careful, not get too frantic."

Cal was hyperventilating. "Okay, I'll tell them." He started for the door again.

"And Cal…"

He turned back. "Yeah?"

"Is there anyone here that might be able to help you?"

He froze. "Help me what?"

"Deliver the baby, of course."

Chapter Nineteen

Holy freezing crap! A baby.

Cal opened the door to the mudroom, slipped out, and had to grab it against the wind. Driving snow hit his face like stinging nettles. He'd donned the first coat he saw and an old pair of boots. The coat didn't quite close. He was freezing. Least of his worries. Would Eli still be there?

Crap. The rapidly piling drifts pulled at his boots as he struggled toward the guesthouse. Surely Eli would have left as soon as the snow started. Hell, he drove a motorcycle.

He pushed open the guesthouse door. He could have cried when he felt the warmth. From a space heater, maybe? Good sign. "Eli? Are you here? Please, I need your help!"

The man came around the corner in a rush. "What is it?" He grabbed Cal's forearms. "Are you in trouble? What's happening?"

Oh man, he could have kissed him, because he was just so *there*. No hesitation, no reservation. Of course, that might change when he heard what was really wrong. "Emmaline, Dr. Silvay, has gone into labor and says the baby is coming fast. Angel has the flu and can't be near her. The guys aren't here." He stared at the beautiful face. Realization was dawning. "She's gonna need help and that leaves me…and you, if you'll help me."

"Holy shit."

"Yep. Who better to deliver a baby than two gay men?" He burst out laughing, and after a beat, Eli laughed too. It felt good. Didn't change anything, but laughing was a relief. "C'mon."

Eli grabbed his coat, turned off the space heater and lights, and fell in behind Cal.

Cal looked over his shoulder. "Why did you stay when you saw the snow? All the other guys were smart enough to leave."

He grinned. "Too stubborn. I wanted to get this done. I figured I could just sleep here in the guesthouse if it got too bad."

"Now you're stuck."

"Yeah, stuck delivering a baby. Think I can put that on my résumé?"

"Only if we do a good job."

Cal used his big feet to make a trail in the drifts for Eli to follow. The wind still blew through his inadequate coat.

They got inside, stamped off the snow on the mudroom floor, tossed their coats, and headed for the stairs. Wasn't he supposed to boil water or something? Later.

He glanced at Eli. "I'll introduce you to Em; then one of us better wake the critter, because we're going to need her expertise in a big way."

He tapped on the master bedroom door. Em's voice sounded winded. "C'mon in, Cal."

The sight was just as mystifying as the last time. Em was on hands and knees on the carpet, belly pointed at the floor, taking deep breaths.

Cal moved up beside her and knelt. "Are you okay?"

"Just helping the baby lock in position and taking a little pressure off my back." She looked up and somehow managed to extend a hand, making her a three-legged turtle. "Hi, I'm Em. You must be Eli."

He knelt down beside Cal and took her hand with a bemused smile. "Yes, ma'am."

"Oh please, dear. You're about to get to know me rather intimately, and it will never work if you call me ma'am."

Eli laughed. "Got it. Glad to meet you, Em. Now what should we do to help you?"

She started doing a gently rocking motion. "Actually, aside from everything happening a bit more quickly than I'd anticipated, things are going well so far."

"I guess you'd know, being a scientist and all." He grinned at her.

"Well, decades of science training and nine months of birthing classes that my guys insisted we take religiously. It was interesting watching the other moms react when I had a different guy with me on alternate weeks. They constantly warred between shock and envy." She laughed, which turned into a series of pants.

Cal waited for her contraction to ebb, then sat on the bed.

She smiled tightly. "I called again just so the guys wouldn't worry too much. I got Roan. I figured he's the master of transportation. He's figuring out how to get the two of them home." Her words trailed off, and she grimaced again.

"I'm going to go wake Angel. She'll be able to guide us through what we need to do, right?"

Em gasped again. "Yes, although if she's not up to it, I've got a pretty good idea of the plan. I've just never done it before, so I can't...ouch...claim to be an expert."

Cal stood up. "I'll go." He looked at Eli. Would he be comfortable with this very pregnant woman he just met?

As Cal watched, Eli settled onto the floor next to Em. "You mentioned your back. Would you like me to rub it?"

Em took a deep breath and let it out noisily. "Hell's bells, beautiful one, for a back rub I might give you my firstborn child, and in light of the circumstances, that's a pretty serious offer."

He laughed, rose up on his knees, and began a slow stroke over her back. "Can't we make you more comfortable?"

"I could get on the bed and support this baby belly."

"Sounds good." As Cal left, Eli was helping her up onto the big bed. Shit, who'd have guessed he was Nurse Eli?

He rushed to the guest bedroom that had been his and Angel's — and Eli's. Peeking inside, he found one concerned female sitting up in bed. "What's going on? I hear you clomping around."

"And I thought I was being quiet."

"Not likely, Mr. Size Thirteen. What's up? Em's in labor, isn't she?"

He breathed out. "Yes, and it seems like the baby is coming fast. Or that's what she says."

She threw her legs over the side of the bed. "Okay. Get my bag over there." She gestured toward the closet.

He held her back. "Wait, you shouldn't be up, and you can't be near her."

She gave him a look, all business. "I know that, *Dr.* Martin, but you can get me closer so I can talk to Em through the door." She gestured to a big plush chair by the fireplace. "Put that in the hall, and I'll bring my blankets. I can't handle any of the equipment, so you'll have to do that. Grab the chair and get back to Em."

"Actually Eli's with her. Last I saw, he was rubbing her back. She promised to give him the baby in return."

He said it with a straight face, and it took her a second to catch on; then she laughed. "Well, I'll be damned. The man is an enigma. Okay, grab the chair, come back for the bag, and get to work."

Cal rushed through the next hour getting Angel settled onto her "throne" outside what they now called the birthing room. The critter issued orders like the pro she was at the same time she called encouragement to Em. It took some trial and error, but Eli attached a fetal heart monitor while Cal laid out packages of instruments that included some serious-looking umbilical scissors and cord clampers beside the basics, like gauze pads and lubricant. They pulled out a thin plastic cloth Em had standing by, and some old sheets she'd already set aside. Through it all, Em walked the room holding her belly like the baby was already there.

Man, Eli was a marvel. Cal thought of himself as well coordinated, but Eli had the manual dexterity of a fine woodworker. He handled the monitors and instruments like a veteran. Yeah, and he didn't even shy away from the girlie bits. He ran a bath for Em and carefully helped her into a few inches of body-temperature water after Angel announced that she was far enough along that the water wouldn't stop her contractions. Em didn't seem to mind Eli seeing her nude. Guess that was the least of her worries right now.

The contractions got closer together, and Eli got calmer. Or at least that's how he appeared. Em seemed soothed just being around him. Cal too. Jesus, the guy was so skittish about relationships, yet here he was up to his ass in the most intimate situation a person could imagine and, seemingly, right at home.

They had set up a delivery center, as Angel called it, in the center of the room, with the plastic cloth and old sheets laid out, the big exercise ball for Em to hold onto, and lots of cushions and pillows of various sizes. Em came out of her bath with her nightgown back on and squatted down, using the ball for balance. Eli rehooked the monitor.

Angel waved a hand at him from the hall. "Cal, you get behind her and support her."

Okay, here we go. He took a deep breath and sat on the floor with his back against a big, heavy chair. Em leaned against him, squatting and steadying herself on the ball. Eli sat beside her on the floor.

Cal had positioned Angel so Em could see her through the open bedroom door. Angel was wrapped up like a cocoon, and alternately sweating and shivering, but she was hanging in there like a champ. She'd been on the phone to Em's doctor three times, just reporting progress, and the doc seemed satisfied that everything was going well. Of course, Angel hadn't told her all the details. As far as the doc knew, Angel was delivering the baby, not two male novices.

Unnnnhhh. Cal listened to the deep, moaning sounds Em made and let them flow through his body the way Angel told Em to let it flow through hers. At first he'd cringed with every contraction. Now he felt like his body was absorbing some of the pain, pulling it from Em. God, she was a trouper. Controlling her breathing, letting the sounds she made carry her through what he knew must be intense pains again and again. Timeless. Everything seemed to exist outside of the natural world, and yet it felt so real. Like he'd never known real life before. Moan. Pant. Moan. Pant. Timeless.

Minutes passed -- or maybe it was hours. He wasn't sure. His back hurt. It didn't hurt. He wanted it to be over. He never wanted it to end. Suspended. All that felt real was the vibration of Em's deep sounds.

He looked up at the sound of Angel's voice. "Em, talk to me. Do you feel like you want to push?"

"Yeah." Em gasped. "I feel like I'm holding back."

"Okay, sweetie, go for it. Cal, hang on to her."

Shit, he was terrified, but so honored to get to do this. Would he ever repeat this for a baby of his own? Wasn't likely, but he'd think about that later.

And then it began. It was like being absorbed into some hole in the universe where nothing else was going on, no worries, no conflicts, no time or space. He was aware of Em's panting and the deep sounds of her cries as she pushed, rested, pushed again. He heard Eli's encouragement, saw him wiping her brow and dabbing water on her lips. He heard Angel calling, "Can you see the baby? Can you see the crown?" The pushes increased. The intensity was unbelievable…and unbearable. How could she do it? How did women do it? Somewhere in the background, in some other universe, he heard a door open and close, but all that was really happening was one huge cry as her body strained against him, and then suddenly relaxed. Smells and sounds, and he saw Eli put a tiny, waxlike doll on Em's chest, still connected to its life-giving cord. Angel called instructions, and Em gently patted the infant. Chills ran through him as he heard the sound of that one first, perfect, unfathomable breath.

"It's a girl." Tears were running down Eli's face, but he didn't seem to notice.

And then came rushing and noise, and Jake and Roan burst through the door, instantly quieted, and surrounded the woman they loved and their perfect, dark-haired daughter.

Cal rolled to the side and surrendered his position to Jake, as Roan gloved and prepared to cut the cord. Jeez. His legs barely worked. But it was worth it. He stood. Oops. Wobbled, caught himself, and moved to the door. Eli was already there watching, his cheeks still wet.

Cal closed the door behind them. The family needed their time to bond. Hey, that new little girl was his family too. He loved that.

Angel was curled in the chair, sound asleep. He looked up at Eli. No words could describe how he felt. He took one step closer. Oh please. Eli grabbed him and pulled his head down. Yes, prayer answered. He welcomed that soft questing tongue into his mouth. Nothing else existed. Like with the birth that they had shared. Cal couldn't suck hard enough or hold Eli tight enough to show how much the moment meant.

When they finally pulled apart, Cal gently caressed Eli's beautiful face. "Thank you. Thank you for being here, for being so great. Thank you for sharing this."

Eli gazed at him a moment, then looked away. "We better get the sleeping critter to bed. She did yeoman work here today."

Okay, end of the moment. "Yeah, she did. I can take her, then come back and help with the chair."

"No, let me carry her." Eli reached down and lifted her into his arms. The guy wasn't much taller than Angel, but he carried her with ease in those strong carpenter's arms. Cal hoisted the chair and brought it behind Eli into the bedroom they had shared for a few nights. As he positioned the chair, he saw Angel's head lift from Eli's shoulder. "Hi, ma beaute."

He gave her a grin. "Hi, cutie."

"I missed you so bad." Her head plopped again on his shoulder. He frowned for a second, then smiled as he gently placed her on the bed and covered her.

Cal looked up at a soft tap on the doorjamb. Roan came into the room.

"Cal, Eli, I just want to thank you both from the bottom of my heart. Jake does too. It was an amazing thing you did. And of, course, the angel there."

Cal smiled. "She's out. But what a trouper."

"Yeah. Look, you guys won't see much of us until tomorrow when the nanny comes. I've called her, so she'll be here early. Meanwhile, Jake and I are putting all our baby classes to work tonight."

"Do you have a name?"

He grinned. "Yeah, I think so, but I won't tell you till we're all together." He turned to Eli. "Eli, I know this wasn't what you signed up for, and I can't thank you enough. If you ever need a recommendation or a testimonial…"

Eli smiled. "As a midwife?"

"Yeah, that too. Okay, you guys have everything you need?"

Cal punched Roan lightly on the arm. "Hey, dad, go on back to your family. We're fine."

He beamed. "Family. Like the sound of that. See you tomorrow."

He ducked out, and they heard the door to the master bedroom close a few seconds later.

Neither of them had moved, Cal beside the chair and Eli next to the bed. Eli said, "Do they know who the father is?"

"No. I don't imagine they'll ever find out."

"That's funny, considering they're geneticists."

"Yeah, but both men are the father no matter whose sperm swam the fastest."

He gazed at a spot on the carpet. "That's nice."

"Eli?"

The gold eyes finally met Cal's. "Yeah?"

"Will you fuck me?"

"Oh shit, yeah." He covered the space in two steps and grabbed Cal's head. It was like the kiss they had shared earlier had just been interrupted. Cal grabbed the smaller man and lifted him from the floor. Eli wrapped his legs tight around Cal's waist and ground their hard cocks together.

Crap, in all the angst, he'd forgotten how good it felt. He grasped Eli's butt and worked him against his own straining erection.

Eli pulled back and looked around the room. "Where can we go so we don't wake the critter?"

A little voice came from the bed. "Don't you dare leave me out of this. I might still be sick, but I'm not blind. I wanna watch."

No more encouragement required. Cal carried Eli to the opposite side of the bed, dumped him on his back, and grabbed the cargo pants at the waist, ripping the button from its hole and dragging down the zipper. As he pulled the rough fabric down those lean legs, Eli's gorgeous pink cock sprang out.

A sound came from among the covers. "Mmm. Pretty."

Eli leaned his head back to look at Angel, who was wholly cocooned in bedding but for that cute face. "You like that, baby?" She nodded her head in the affirmative. "So what do you want to watch?"

"Want to watch him suck. He's really good at it." Man, that sounded good.

"Yep, he is." He looked down toward Cal. "Hear that, big guy? You don't want to disappoint the little lady."

Cal dragged his T-shirt over his head. "Hell no. I'd never disappoint the angel of mercy." Crap. He wanted that cock. He flopped onto the mattress beside Eli, grabbed that leaking dick, and took an experimental lick. Just as sweet and salty as he remembered. "Is that what you want, Angel? My tongue on this pretty pink cock?"

"No, I want to see how far down your throat you can get that baby before you gag."

"Oh shit." Apparently Eli liked the idea.

All compliance, Cal did an "open mouth, insert cock" move and then swallowed.

"Oh shiiiit." Yep. Eli definitely liked the idea.

"God, suck it, Cal, suck it. " Angel reached down under the covers, and he could see the covers moving. Jesus, her masturbating just made this better and better.

Eli glanced up at the movement. "You getting off, baby?"

"Hell yeah. Can't let you have all the fun."

"Come over here and let me eat you."

"Naw, I'll freeze outside these covers, and I don't want to get you sick. But I am going to want to see some fucking real soon."

Just listening to those two talk dirty had Cal ready to come. He sucked deep, and Eli lifted off the mattress, moaning.

She was loving egging them on. "You gonna let the big guy top you, Eli, or are you going to ream that beautiful ass for him?"

Eli could barely talk. "Uh, what do you want…?"

"You fuck him, ma beaute. He loves it so much."

Man, was it that obvious that he was a bottom? At least he was for Eli.

"You got it." In one move, Eli rose up to sitting, pulled Cal's head away from his cock by his hair, and gave him a searing kiss, then pulled away, still gripping his hair. "Oh yeah, I taste me. You like how I taste?"

"I do."

"You wanna be fucked, don't you? Your pretty ass is clenching right now for my cock, isn't it?"

Cal nodded, a little embarrassed by Angel's intense observation.

"I didn't hear you. Do you want me to fuck you?"

"Yes, Eli."

"You worried about your Angel hearing you beg? Is that your problem?" Cal didn't respond. "But she loves hearing her big guy beg, don't you, Angel? You wanna hear him plead a little, don't you?"

"Hell yes. Beg for it, mon grand. See how much you excite me. Merde, my pussy is so wet I can hardly feel my fingers. I have to get well real quick so I can have your big, big cock in me. But right now, I want to see how much you love getting fucked. Show me. Beg him. Beg."

The top of his head was coming off. He couldn't think, only feel, and his whole body burned for Eli. "Please, Eli, please."

Eli unbuttoned Cal's jeans and pulled them off. "Please what, baby? What do you want?"

"Fuck me."

"What else?"

"Put your cock in me."

"What else?"

"Oh shit!" Cal struggled over onto his hands and knees. He put his butt in the air and arms behind his back, balancing on his head. "Hold me down and ream me. Fuck me till I can't see and don't care. Own me, Eli."

One strong, rough hand grabbed Cal's wrists, and the other pushed lube into the hottest, most aching hole on the planet. Cal knew he was making a high keening noise, but he couldn't stop.

Eli shoved in a second finger. Cal felt like he could take the whole fist. "Doesn't he ask pretty? I think I gotta give him what he wants." With a yank, Cal pulled Eli's arms back and rammed his cock straight into his ass. Then he went to town. No gradual buildup, no finesse. He started pounding like a pile driver, hitting Cal's gland on almost every stroke. "This what you want? Is this good, Angel?"

Cal's face pressed into the blanket, but he could feel the vibration of Angel's flying fingers and hear her high-pitched little cries as she got closer to orgasm. "You're gorgeous. I wish I'd known years ago how much I love watching men fuck. You're hot. So hot. Oh oh oh."

Cal knew she was coming, and it just made him hotter, if that was possible. His cock rubbed hard against the covers, the friction driving him mad. Sex was all he could smell; Eli was all he could feel. All he wanted to feel.

Eli's hips were pistons as Cal flew closer and closer to the sun. "Crap, you feel good. I hate how much I love fucking you. You make me never want to stop fucking. Cal, Cal, I... Oh God."

The thought of Eli coming in his ass pushed the last known button. "Eli. I love you." For a moment, Cal cringed at what he had said, but what the hell? The truth was important tonight. *Sheee-it.* Hot cum bubbled from his balls and seared out his cock onto the bedding, pump after pump, each one pushing another bolt of heat through his groin, up his spine, and into his head. Dizzy. Thought he would pass out from pure pleasure. Pure Eli.

In the silence that followed, Cal savored the weight of Eli on his back and the soft sounds of Angel's breath in sleep. She'd said he would only be happy if he had a male lover. Crap. Why did she always have to be right?

Chapter Twenty

Cal opened his eyes. First impression? Stuck to the bed in his own dried cum. Second impression? No lean male body next to him. He heard Angel's gentle breath, but that was it. He didn't even have to look. He'd known in his sleep. Eli was gone.

He pulled his nude body away from the dried patch on the blanket and sat up. Pieces of semen stuck to the chest that never had been able to grow much hair. What a mess.

He looked around at the soft light filtering through the curtains. The real mess wasn't on his chest. Here he sat, no certainty how he wanted to live his life, in love with a woman who was leaving him, in love with a man who already had. Hot pressure behind his eyes made him mad. He wasn't going to cry. That would be stupid. He had to take the action open to him and surrender the shit he couldn't control. He half grinned at his own rather liberal interpretation of St. Francis.

Okay, action and surrender. Which was which?

Eli was gone. Surrender? Oh crap, the tears pushed forward, and he wiped his eyes. He didn't even know where to find him if he wanted to go storm his bastions and try to get the man to love him back. No use. Give up.

Angel? She was leaving too. But she wasn't gone. Maybe a little hope there.

Okay, life path? He hadn't signed that bloody contract. Yet.

"I smell wood burning."

He looked up into those mischievous brown eyes peering over the top of a mound of covers.

She pulled her face out of the pile, and he saw her smile. "Any man thinking that hard could have an accident."

He tried to smile back, but his chest was too tight. "We already did."

"What?"

"Eli's gone."

"Merde. The lily-livered, chickenshit asshole." Her vehemence carried her all the way to sitting, so he got a good look at her blue flannel PJs. "Cal, I'm so damned sorry."

"Don't be sorry for me. You love him too."

She drew a shaky breath. "Yeah, I do. But I loved you first. Not having you broke my heart. Eli just stomped it to pieces."

"Oh shit, critter." He leaned over and gathered her long, slim frame onto his lap. Tears ran down his face, and he tried desperately not to sob. She made no such effort. Her shoulders shook as she buried her face in his neck.

"Cal, I don't know how I can leave you. Even though I know it won't work to give up my life for a man who can't ever give me all of himself, I just don't know how to leave." The sobs continued.

He hugged her close. "I know. I can't bear to lose you either."

Gradually, her sobs became little sighs. "I loved being close to you last night, working together to get that baby born."

"God, last night was like a dream for me. I've never felt so at peace, so at one with you and Eli and Em. It felt right, being at the center of some kind of real human experience, you know? Helping someone who needed help. Touching and being touched. Not just a game."

"Doesn't that give you your answer about signing that contract?"

Jesus. "Maybe it does. I keep thinking about the reasons why I should or shouldn't sign. Maybe the bottom line is how I feel?"

She leaned back and looked at his face. "Duh. You may be gay, but you're such a guy."

He sighed and set her back on the bed. "Not sure that changes anything. No matter how I feel, the situation is fucked. How are you feeling?"

She gave him a sideways glance at his change of subject. "Hmmf. I'm actually feeling better. I guess birthing babies and getting off while watching beautiful men have sex is the new antiflu drug. Think we can offer the patent to big pharma?" She rubbed idly at her dripping nose.

"I want to see the clinical trials." He got up, still naked, and started toward the bathroom. "I'll get cleaned up and get you some breakfast. I imagine the family has a few other distractions."

"Yeah. I'll still have to stay away from Em and the baby. I can't wait to see her. Is she gorgeous?"

"Hell, consider the sources. While my brother is one great-looking dude, I'll bet he secretly hopes it was Roan's sperm that won out. Imagine a girl that looks like Roan. Sheee-it."

"That could be more than the population can stand."

"Kind of like if you had a baby by me and Eli, I'd want it to be Eli that was the father, since he'd make such a pretty girl." The words were out. No take backs. They stared at each other. Stricken. He turned toward the shower.

Angel stared after him for a minute, watching those wide shoulders and narrow hips. Gorgeous. God, she loved him. There had to be choices here, like Shakti had said. There had to be a way out that didn't suck. Dieu, there was such talent, so many brains and resources in this family. They couldn't be without options… Sheee-it, as Cal would say. Maybe…?

Idea! She hopped out of bed. *Whoa. Hold on.* She grabbed the dresser to keep from falling over. Oh, yes, she was sick. So what? She rummaged through her clothes for a pair of sweats, one step in formality above her PJs, found a cold mask in her bag and put it on, then stopped to glance in the mirror. Hair in several directions, eyes a bit bleary, and a mask over nose and mouth. That should scare old people and small children. Oh well, not to be helped.

As she opened the bedroom door, she heard the shower from the bathroom. She hoped he took his time. Padding down the stairs, she heard wonderful sounds of domesticity. A baby gurgling and squalling and the laughs and funny cooing sounds big humans seemed to make whenever a baby was around.

She rounded the corner into the great room. They didn't hear her because both men were riveted on Em, curled on the couch, covered in blankets, and the little bundle she had attached to her chest.

Angel grinned. "I'm sure I don't have to ask if she's the most beautiful baby on earth."

All eyes raised, she thought reluctantly, to her. Em waved a hand. "Hi, darling. I'm so sorry you're sick, and so grateful for all you and your team of beautiful boys did for me. How are you feeling?"

Angel waved a hand. Had to get some things accomplished before Cal came down. "Well enough. How's the nursing going? Is she latching on?"

"Oh, yes, dear. Antonia is helping so much." She gestured to a youngish, black-haired woman who had just walked in from the kitchen.

Ah yes, the nanny. "Great. Antonia, I'll want to talk to you later on today, if I may, but right now I need Roan and Jake, and I need them quick."

Em frowned. "Is something wrong?"

"Actually, I hope to make something right, but I need the guys to make it work."

Roan and Jake both got up from their positions on the floor beside Em and the baby. Jake pointed down the hall. "How about in the office?"

"Good."

She practically ran down the hall, and the men followed at what she thought was a snail's pace. Finally they were all seated around one of the three desks that occupied the big, book-lined office. Jake sat in the desk chair, looking at home. This must be his spot. Roan and she sat in the guest chairs.

She glanced at the door. Cal could be here any minute. "Before I say anything else, I want to make something clear. I'm in love with Caleb. I know it's insane. My life is all about my work, and he's fundamentally a gay man, but those are the facts."

Roan caught on quick. "What about Elijah?"

That ice pick would never come out of her heart. "He's gone. I don't imagine we'll see him again." She looked up at Roan's clear green eyes. "Yeah, maybe there was a way to make it all work if he'd stayed. Like you three. But could you have lived your life in a heterosexual relationship and been happy?"

The beautiful man shook his head. "I honestly don't know. My love for Em is unequivocal, but it's so tied up with my love for Jake that I can't separate the two. I once considered a life with a woman and backed away."

Jake chimed in. "But she wasn't Em."

"Yes, true."

Angel sighed. "Anyway, I think I'm prepared to stay in the States and do my work in order to give a relationship with Cal a chance. I can do some work for Global Outreach in New York, maybe work out of the headquarters building."

Jake frowned. "Will that make you happy?"

"It will be hard. And most of all, it doesn't solve Cal's problems. It maybe just makes them worse."

Jake sat forward. "In what way?"

"He'll just blame himself for taking away my life's work, and you know how he is about that."

"Yeah."

Roan flashed his brilliant, crooked-tooth smile. "Actually I've been toying with an idea for a couple of days, and I think I can make it work."

She smiled back. "Good, because I've got an idea too, and I wouldn't be surprised if they go together."

He cocked his head. "First, confirm something. I have the feeling that Cal doesn't really want to sign that contract. Do you think that's true?"

"I know it's true. And now he knows it too, but I think he's planning on signing because he feels there's no way out."

Roan sat forward and leaned his elbows on his knees, hands clasped. "Okay, then, let's talk about ways out."

*****

Cal gazed down at the infant. "Oh my God, Em, she's gorgeous." The tiny girl, just a bit shy of seven pounds, had a solid head of soft dark hair and eyes that now looked like a deep blue. Em assured him that babies' eyes changed color, but he knew that baby would have Roan's dark hair and the Martin blue eyes, thereby confounding anyone who tried to guess her biological father. Speaking of whom, Cal glanced around the big room, bright with early morning sun. "Where are the guys? Where's Angel? She wasn't in her bed when I came out of the shower."

Em patted her baby, who was beginning to look like she needed some posterior attention. "They're all down in the office. I expect you'd be welcome if you want to join them." Em gestured to the nanny, who came over and took the baby while Em got out from under the covers. "I think we should change her, Antonia."

Okay. She was in mommy world. What the hell was going on down the hall?

Cal walked down the polished floors and tapped on the closed door. Odd.

"Come in." Jake's voice. When he walked in, Angel was on her cell phone, Roan hung on the landline, and Jake was smiling from behind his desk. "Hey, big guy, c'mon in. We've got some thoughts we want to discuss with you."

"What's up?" He walked over to the couch beside the desk and sat. Angel disconnected her cell. Roan gestured for them to wait for him, then hung up. He turned to Cal.

"Angel tells us you don't want to sign the contract. Is that for sure?"

"Hey, it's not a problem. I can play. It's the easiest thing to do. All the hassle will go away." Shit, it did not feel good to say that.

Jake leaned forward at the desk. "Cal, this is grown-up time. You're making choices that affect a lot of people, not the least of them you. Tell the truth."

He ran a hand through his hair. "I don't want to sign, Jake. I know I'm an ungrateful asshole, but I want to do something more. I want to make a difference."

"Like what? What do you want to do?"

Cal threw himself against the back of the couch. "I don't know."

Roan's soft voice cut in. "Dream, Cal. What would you do if you could do anything?"

He shook his head. "I can't even think like that. It could hurt Angel and her organization."

Angel smiled softly. "Tell us, mon grand. What would you do?"

Wow. What would he do? The words rushed out. "I'd do something like you do, Angel. Go somewhere the need is huge. Help people. Change the world one person at a time." Hell yes. That's what he'd do. "Like when you talked about the people in Senegal who get mistreated because they're gay or have AIDS. It's not right. Who's helping them? Tell me that?"

Angel smiled. "Maybe you are."

Chapter Twenty-one

A few fast-moving New Yorkers brushed past him as he looked up at the old high-rise. This was it. Tomorrow was the press conference. A lot to do. A lot to try and make work. Could he do it? There had been several phone conferences and online meetings the last two days, but this was the big event. When he left here today, his life would either be on a whole new track, or he'd be cannon fodder for Elias Dante.

It was weird to feel excited, terrified, and kicked in the teeth all at the same time. Shit, he should get used to it. The rip in his heart that was Eli felt like a dripping wound. Would it go away? Yeah, with time he'd have a permanent scar. Right now, standing here, it was hard to think he wasn't kicking Eli back.

He kicked at a bottle someone had left on the sidewalk. Definitely not a fashionable part of town. *Take a deep breath, man.* If they all said yes, the world would change -- including every jealously guarded moment of the life of the man he loved.

* * * * *

Cal sat on the dais in the big hotel ballroom behind a table with microphones placed every few feet. Members of the press crowded the space below him. His shoulder brushed against Whitaker, the team owner, on one side. Morales, the goalie, sat on the other, looking robust and healthy, thank God. Beyond Whitaker, Cal could feel more than see Elias Dante. Jesus, his arrogance shimmered in the air like heat lightning. Other members of the team were seated past him.

Dante was so sure of himself he'd simply asked Cal if he had the contract with him. Cal assured him he did. It made him smile, even if he wanted to barf from nerves. At the moment, a reporter was asking Whitaker about the starting lineup. He'd just explained the midfielders and forward. "And our starting goalie will be --"

Cal grabbed his mike. "A hale and hearty Pedro Morales, the greatest goalie the league has ever had." Morales beamed, and the press applauded wildly. Cal looked over at the owner. "Sorry to steal your thunder, Mr. Whitaker. I'm just excited Pedro is doing so great."

A crease appeared between Whitaker's brows. "That's okay, Cal. Of course, with you behind him, Pedro will be twice as strong."

Cal took a deep breath. Game on. "Actually, sir, I have an announcement that I'm pretty excited about. If I may." He didn't wait for permission. He picked up the microphone and stood with it in his hand. He hoped the press couldn't see him shake. "Some of you may be aware that my college degree is in sociology. It only seemed like I majored in soccer." A few chuckles from the crowd. "And my family is very much involved in the helping professions. It's always been a dream of mine to follow in their footsteps. I just hadn't found my path."

That high nasal voice interrupted. "Cal, you should think --"

Cal rushed on. "Well, very recently I've received an offer that gives me the chance I've waited for. The chance of a lifetime. You probably know that Mr. Dante is a big supporter of a nonprofit organization called Global Outreach." Cal turned toward Dante, who was glaring daggers at him. "It turns out that, amazingly enough, the woman I love works for this organization in Africa. And my brother-in-law, Roan Black, also supports this organization through his foundation. They do such fine work, Roan Black's Model World Foundation is challenging Mr. Dante and other contributors to raise a half billion dollars to extend their life-saving programs." He glanced at Dante with a smile. *Oh yeah, I'm sure that delights you, you bastard. Hah. Gotcha.* "Anyway, this organization that helps so many people around the world with health care has asked me to head up a new program in Senegal, working to improve the health opportunities for those who have least access to it. This will give me the chance to work directly with people in a serving capacity, as I've always dreamed." He grinned. "And, of course, be with the woman I love."

He sat back down to dead silence. A flash went off. Then another. Several reporters fired questions at the same time. Whitaker leaned over, covering the mike. "You might have warned me, Cal."

Cal looked at the man. He really liked him, even if he had become a tool of Dante's. "Sorry, sir, it literally just happened, and frankly, I didn't want to give Dante much warning to try and derail my plans."

Whitaker stared at him a moment. Cal watched a war behind his eyes. He was losing his goalie, a chunk of his livelihood. Finally the dad in him seemed to win. "I understand, son. I want you to have a happy life. I hope you know that." He reached out and shook Cal's hand. Flashes sparked around the room.

A woman reporter stood up. "I just want to say on behalf of my publication that the people of America will be proud of you. It's not often we see someone willing to give up fame to go work in the trenches."

Cal smiled. "Thank you."

"Cal. Oh, Cal." A lot of voices were raised, but Cal recognized that snarky tabloid reporter's voice. Might as well get it over with.

"Yes." He nodded at the guy, since he wasn't sure of his name.

"Cal, aren't you really quitting soccer because you're gay and you can't stand the harassment you get from the *real* men on the teams? Isn't your so-called 'woman you love' just a fag-hag cover-up?"

Several of the other reporters were booing.

"Give it up."

"Not this again."

Cal stood up. Real deep breath time. "The woman I love is very real." Another breath. "However, prior to this time, most of my significant relationships have been with men. I suppose you would say I'm bisexual."

Again there was a slight lull before the furor broke out.

"What do your teammates think of having a gay goalie?"

"What do you think of this, Whitaker?"

"How bad has the harassment been?"

Cal lifted the mike to try and answer and simply froze. Walking up the center aisle of the big room was a vision so beautiful, it made his mouth dry. Slim, perfectly dressed in an immaculate black suit, white shirt, and red tie, golden curls unfurled around his shoulders, was Eli. As Cal gazed, the reporters became aware of the intruder and likewise stared. Questions -- "Who is that? Why is he here?" -- rushed through the group. Cal just had to smile. He really didn't care why he was here. Just seeing that face was enough.

Eli walked to the side and up onto the dais. He grabbed the nearest microphone. "I'm so sorry to interrupt." Cal glanced at Dante. The man's expression was somewhere between angry and bemused. He looked back at Eli. Even with his father in the room, Eli commanded attention -- that special charisma along with the spectacular beauty.

"Most of you don't know me. I'm the man you often call the prodigal son, the missing child, the mystery man. I'm Elijah Dante."

The place went nuts. Cameras, questions. Eli looked completely calm. He pointed to a reporter in the front row.

"Where have you been, Elijah?"

He smiled that Botticelli angel smile. "I live a very quiet existence. I enjoy working with my hands, and I'm pleased to say that my father has made it possible for me to remain private and live my life out of the public eye."

Oh, the tricky devil. Giving his father credit for his manipulation.

"Why are you here?"

He looked over toward Cal and smiled. "Mr. Martin told you, prior to his current relationship, most of his partners were men. I was one of those."

The past tense made Cal's chest hurt. The reporters went super nuts! They couldn't ask questions fast enough. Eli held up his hand. The place quieted.

"I'm simply here today to show my support for Caleb's decision. I know how much my father has wanted Cal to remain with the team." He looked at his father and smiled what could have been a smile of admiration. Yeah, right. That's what triumph looked like. "You see, having a homosexual son has made my dad an advocate. I'm sure he believes strongly that Cal is an asset to the team and to football in general, and that the sport should embrace all its players regardless of their race, creed, ethnicity or…sexual orientation. I'm sure he wants Cal to show the world that a great player can be straight or gay as long as he can block a kick.

"But I know that's not what Cal is meant to do. There aren't a lot of truly giving and selfless people in this world. We can't afford to waste one of them. I hope his whole team and all the members of the press will respect and honor his choice. I know it hasn't been easy for him." He grinned. "He's had a lot of pressure from all sides, but I'm in awe of his choices." He laughed. "Okay, enough of that sentimental crap. Let's let the man get on with his life. I'll bet the team has some great news about the coming season."

He started to leave the dais. One reporter shouted, "Are you and Cal still an item? What about the girlfriend? Is that just a smoke screen?"

Eli stopped and stared at the reporter. Those gold eyes would have cowed a linebacker. "No, sadly, life tore Cal and me apart. And I know his girlfriend personally. She's wonderful, and I'm very happy for them. That's all."

He started walking down the steps. Cal fell in behind him. The reporters kept shouting and started to crowd toward the front to follow them, but some hotel security guards stepped in. Cal grabbed Eli's arm. "This way."

He slipped through a back door of the ballroom used by staff and into a corridor that took them to the kitchen.

Eli smiled. "You must have scoped this out in advance."

Cal looked over his shoulder, still leading Eli by the hand. "Oh yeah."

After winding through some carts of food supplies, they made it to a dark vestibule used for deliveries. Cal stopped and turned to Eli. "I have Roan's town car and driver outside. Need a ride?" He held his breath.

"No, thanks. I have the bike near here."

Cal pointed to the beautiful suit. "You traveling like that?"

"No, I've got some leathers stashed."

Cal brought his hand up and caressed the beautiful face. "Why did you do it, Eli? You told me you were going to run. I took you at your word. Why did you come here today?"

Eli put his hand over Cal's. For a second, Cal felt rejected, but then Eli pressed closer. "I came to hear your decision. I had no idea you would use his plot so thoroughly against him. It was inspiring, and I had to get in on it." He grinned. "But regardless of what you said today, I intended to reveal myself to the press. I wanted to eliminate one of his sources of leverage over you. In the name of protecting my freedom, I've put myself in his cage and handed him the key. I realized I'd never be free as long as I was terrified of somebody invading my privacy. So here I am, making a spectacle of myself."

Eli dropped his hand, and Cal followed suit, reluctantly. "Thanks. I'm really grateful."

"So you're going to Africa. Wow. What a great solution."

"Yeah. It's a terrific opportunity. I didn't tell the whole story in there, because I don't want it to hit the news. Gay men are really oppressed in Senegal. So much so that they don't get good health care and end up putting their own lives and those of their partners in danger." Cal felt his chest swell. God, he was excited. "I'm setting up facilities that will tacitly be general health care, but we'll quietly put out there that gay men are welcome and their identities will be kept secret. I want to offer mental as well as physical help."

"Shit. Sounds dangerous, Cal."

"I won't lie. It's not going to be a picnic, but Global Outreach says they'll work to protect us. And Jesus, Eli, think of how bad those men's lives must be. Crap. Somebody has to help."

Eli laughed. "Yeah, this is what you're meant to do, all right."

"What will you do?"

"For now, go back to Vermont. See what the press does after this. See what my clients do when they read about this in the paper, when they know the truth."

"Where are you spending Thanksgiving?"

He shook his head. "Haven't thought past today."

"You're more than welcome to join us in Connecticut. It's going to be the whole family gathering to see the baby. I know Em would love to thank you." Cal didn't feel much hope.

Eli looked up at him, those steady gold eyes unreadable. "Thanks. Thank Em for me too." He turned toward the door.

"Eli." The man looked back. "I love you."

"Thank you." He walked out the door.

Cal took a deep breath. That was that. Would he ever get used to the pain in his heart? Yeah, he had Angel, and, oh God, he had Africa. The thrill consumed him.

He walked out into the cold, crisp sunshine, snow slushing on the ground. Roan's car waited with his driver, William, hanging out the driver's door. He came around as Cal approached, but Cal waved at him. "I got it, William. You don't have to wait on me."

The good-looking young man laughed. "That sure runs in your family."

Cal reached for the door handle.

"Cal."

That high, nasal voice stopped him. Chill city. He consciously straightened his spine. He had nothing to fear from this man. He turned on Dante with a smile. "Mr. Dante."

The man grinned. "Since you've given me the shaft today, I'd think we could be on a first-name basis."

"That wasn't my intention, sir. I just want to live my life without having you hurt my friends."

"Well, I think you're making a mistake, but I suppose I will concede the field, at least for now. So your brother-in-law is going to better my contributions to Global Outreach?"

"Yes. With a group of other investors."

"Then they're going to be a very rich charity, because I will be continuing my support."

Well, son of a bitch. "Thank you. I'm sure we can put that money to good use."

"Please note the power of that money, Cal. Without it, you can do nothing."

"Yes, but without the people to put it to work, the money is dead."

"So we're still a team. You sure you don't want to work for Dante Enterprises in Africa?"

He never gave up. "Thanks, sir, but I'm happy with my current position."

"I'd pay you better" -- he shook his head -- "but then, you aren't all that excited about money, are you?" He stuck out his hand.

Cal took it after only a second's hesitation. "And what about Eli, sir?"

The man frowned. "I'll have to see about that. The man showed some balls today, and I appreciate balls." He laughed. "Well, maybe not as much as you and Eli."

Cal couldn't help it. He burst out laughing.

"But he's still my son, and I'm sick of his game playing. I want him to get serious about his life."

"He is serious, Elias. That's why he works so hard to escape you."

"Perhaps. He hasn't impressed me yet."

"You're a hard man to impress."

"Well, kid, you've done it. So good luck to you." And he walked back toward the entrance to the hotel.

Cal watched him go, then glanced at William where he waited patiently beside the driver door.

The man nodded. "Everything okay?"

Cal thought of Eli's beautiful face, and his heart hurt. *Okay, switch it up, man.* He pictured that cute, bouncy tomboy waiting for him at home. "Yeah. Pretty okay. Pretty damned okay."

Across the street in the alley, Eli waited by his bike. He was so proud of Cal. Shit, even his father was impressed by the big guy. Going off to do what he loved with someone he loved and risking a lot to do it. Man, what would that be like?

He loved carpentry. Smoothing beautiful wood, watching something take shape. It gave him a thrill. And he loved working with kids. But he'd always had to hide out to do it, and that took the fun out of it. He shrugged. The cat was sure as hell out of the bag now. Was he just going to wait around for the press to find him?

He kicked at a rock. *C'mon, man, that's not really the question, is it? Are you going to give the fuck up and never have somebody to love? Are you going to walk away from the two best things that ever happened to you?* Yeah, well. Shit happens. He straddled the bike and pointed it toward Vermont.

Chapter Twenty-two

Talk about crazy. That defined the two days before Thanksgiving. Roan and Angel were ecstatic to have so many people to cook for. Cal moved his and Angel's stuff into the new guesthouse so that their big room in the house could be given over to the arriving grand dame, Shakti Silvay. The woman was a pack of wonderful clichés, driving from California in a Volkswagen bus, lugging every herb, vitamin, oil, and scented candle in a '60s retrospective.

The press seemed to be at bay. After the press conference, some reporters had tried to follow him, but William had made the drive confusing enough that they gave up. They probably didn't think Cal was all that exciting anymore. Fine by him. The headlines about his sexual orientation had warred with the positive approval of his change of profession for a couple of days, then died down.

The guesthouse was a staging area for the supplies and materials he wanted to take with him to Africa. He and Angel planned how they would set up and quietly promote the new clinics. He hadn't been this excited since early in college, before soccer took over his life. Angel drilled him in French, and then he drilled her in far more fun ways for half the night. His heart was full, if you didn't count the missing piece.

At the house, the clan was gathering. All the Martins would join in on a combination Thanksgiving and baby-welcoming party. Just to escape the confusion for a minute, he'd brought some books on African folklore that Roan had given him down to the guesthouse. He sat on the bed and leafed through the books. There was a gentle tap on the door and then a call, "Cal?"

He smiled. "Hey, Mom, in here."

Cal was always amazed at how Lydia Martin's slim body and golden hair showed so little of her fifty-plus years. She was his rock and the heart of the family, a hardworking nurse who adored her four children and accepted their quirks and foibles as long as they were happy.

"Hey, baby."

He stood up and hugged his mom, which required some serious bending from his six feet five to her five-four. "You tracking me down?"

"I wanted to tell you that hors d'oeuvres are being set out as we speak, and I think Emmaline is revving up for some kind of big announcement."

He laughed. "Maybe she's finally going to tell us the name the three of them selected for the baby. Hell, they've been calling her 'baby girl' for six days."

"She sure is beautiful."

"Ha. What did you expect with Emmaline and those two fathers?"

"I guess they're never going to find out whose sperm did the job, are they?"

"They don't care."

"Yes. When I discovered they really meant that, I was very proud. It takes a lot of love to suppress the male desire to claim his offspring as his own." She looked at his books. "I'm very proud of you too, dear. I know how you've struggled with what you wanted to do next. Not many men could have walked away from the temptation to be rich and famous." She grinned up at him. He sat on the edge of the bed and patted the space next to him. She settled down. "We better not linger too long, or they'll send the big guns."

"Dad?"

"No, Shakti."

He laughed. His mom and Shakti had become great friends by phone and Facebook, but this was the first time they'd met in person.

"That is a pretty amazing family, isn't it?"

"Yes, and now you have your own stake in that clan, don't you?"

He could feel himself blushing. "Yeah. She's something."

"I adore her, actually. Smart, strong, with Shakti's determination. I think Angel has a lot of Em in her. She's a great addition to your life."

"Thanks, Mom. Is there a 'but'?"

"No, more of an 'and.' She's a great addition, and she's a woman, and you are attracted to men."

"But I am attracted to her, Mom. Actually, she turns me on like a hot water faucet." He blushed again. "Sorry, TMI."

"No, dear, not at all. I'm glad she turns you on. I expect that has something to do with her boyish looks and dominant personality." He looked up at her, startled. His mom's perception never ceased to amaze him. "Sex is important, Cal. It's great that you two want to save the world together, but without that attraction, you're brother and sister."

"Yeah, I know."

"What about the man, Cal?"

Shit.

"Roan told me about him."

"He's gone."

"You love him?"

"He doesn't love me, uh, us back."

"I'm sorry. Are you sure your affection for Angel isn't just rebound from this man? That wouldn't be fair to her."

"No, Mom. I loved her before I knew I loved him."

She stared at him with that see-into-your-soul gaze. "Good. That's what I wanted to know. And I also want to know that you'll be careful. The clinics you're proposing are a dangerous idea in a country where gay men are often killed. Both you and Angel will be at risk."

"I don't have any illusions, Mom. I've talked with the people at Global Outreach. We'll be setting up a very careful cover for the clinics and treating a whole range of people. Plus, they'll provide Angel and me with a lot of protection."

"Good." She patted his hand. "I am proud, Cal. But I'm a mom first. What will you do first when you get there?"

"We have to build a new clinic in Dakar. Wish I'd learned a few skills while I was supervising this guesthouse. They haven't got enough builders, so I'll be picking up a hammer real quick."

"You'll be good at it, baby, just like you are at everything else."

Was he? Wow, what a thought. "Love you." He kissed her nose. "Now let's get up there before Em spills her surprise without us."

They walked arm in arm up to the house, their breath making steam in the cold air. Going in through the French doors, he was hit with an explosion of warmth and merriment. It might be cold and gray outside, but not in the Silvay-Martin-Black residence.

The whole troop was gathered in the great room around the blazing fire. Em held place of honor with Baby Girl in her arms. Jake and Roan flanked her, and Antonia, the nanny, sat beside Jake. Spread around the huge sectional were Shakti, dyed red hair blazing like an early Christmas ornament, seated next to Cal's dad, Burt. The man's big frame dwarfed Shakti's plush but petite body. He was laughing at her. Yep, she was pretty outrageous.

Cal's big brother, Sean, was seated beside Roan and Sean's wife, Anne, and his sister, Jenny, came next. Sean's kids had given up trying to sit still and were playing in the backyard. Angel sat on the end. He could tell she was ready to hop up and replenish food. All kinds of dips, cheeses, vegetables, nuts, and chips were spread out across the big coffee table. The house smelled of cooking turkey and other good things. Behind the gathering, the almost bare trees made architectural patterns against the huge wall of windows.

When they walked in, Shakti made space for Lydia beside Burt, and Cal sat next to Angel. He gave her a squeeze. Conversations played around the table as people reached for their choice morsels.

Em broke into the friendly banter. "Okay, everybody, I don't know how much longer I can keep Baby Girl happy without feeding or changing, so let us officially make our announcement."

Cal laughed. "Are you finally gonna name that child? Did you put Baby Girl on her birth certificate?"

Em snorted. "Yes, we are going to name her, smart aleck. May I have a drumroll, please?"

Sean supplied a pretty effective trilling.

She looked at Jake and Roan excitedly. Roan nodded as if she should go on. "We have decided to name her for the people who brought her into this world." What? What did she mean? "Her name is Kayla Elian Martin-Black."

Shakti leaned forward. "Okay, for those of us who weren't here for the big event…"

Jake laughed. "That would be nearly everybody, Shakti."

"Okay, so explain."

Em beamed. "Kayla was as close as we could get to Caleb, my rock, my support, who held me fast through the birth."

Cal felt tears push up behind his eyes. Aw, shoot, a couple escaped.

"Elian is for Elijah, who kept us all calm through the whole event and made me believe he had delivered a dozen babies, even thought he had just come in from building cabinets." Cal felt another tear fall as the whole night rushed back.

"And Elian is also for our Angel, who commanded the event from her place in the hall, overseeing every detail, even though she was sick as a dog." Em held the baby up. "Ladies and gentlemen, I give you Kayla Elian Martin-Black."

Angel looked up at Cal, tears running down her face too. He grabbed her and hugged her tight. When he released her, she turned and smiled through her tears. "Oh, Em, Jake, Roan, I'm so honored."

Cal croaked, "Me too," which made everyone look at him, and he knew this had to be the king of blushes.

And then Shakti asked the obvious question. "Who's Elijah?"

Cal stared at her. He couldn't answer. He still felt the power of that night. Holding Em's thrashing body, hearing Angel's strong voice leading them while gazing into those golden eyes that assured him everything was as it should be. God, would it ever be as it should be again?

Angel must have seen he was frozen. "He was a friend, a carpenter, who worked on the guesthouse. When we saw that the baby was coming fast, and I was too sick to be near her, Em told Cal to find some help. Eli stepped in, even though he didn't really know Em at all."

Shakti slapped a knee. "Good for him. Sounds like a real man."

Angel squeezed Cal's hand tight. "Yeah, he is."

Em and Antonia took the baby, uh, Kayla, up to the nursery, and the general munching and conversation resumed.

Shakti took a bite of carrot, then gestured with the other half. "So, Cal, Em told me a while back you were gay. How did you and Angel get together?"

You had to love the woman. She would say what everyone was thinking. He decided to be light about it. "Have you ever heard of the idea of 'gay for you'?"

"You mean where a straight guy falls in love with a man, and so becomes gay for that guy? Kind of like Jake and Roan?"

"Yeah. I'm the opposite. I guess you could say I'm 'straight for you.' I'm a gay man who fell in love with a woman."

"Oh, that's great. 'Straight for you.' But actually you're saying you're bisexual, right?"

He hugged Angel to his side. "I doubt I would be for anyone else, but I am for her."

"Well, that's good. I think you make a beautiful couple. I'm glad you'll be in Africa to take care of my girl."

"Me too." Angel went to get more veggies, since the troops were going through them like locusts. Cal leaned over to Sean. "So tell me about the firehouse. How's the new scheduling?"

Sean smiled. "Working fine. But I want to hear about the great birthing event. You gonna become a midwife in Africa? Or maybe take over Mom's job?"

Cal laughed, though the power of that night still lingered. "Actually it was that event that pushed me into my decision. There was so much reality to it. So different than the way I felt on the soccer field. I imagine it's a lot like when you and Dad are in the middle of a fire. Completely present, with no extraneous thoughts. Just doing what you have to do. I loved it."

Sean nodded. "Yeah, that's part of the pull of firefighting, all right." He reached for some food.

Cal heard a motorcycle, and his heart paused. Jesus, how long would that go on?

He turned back to Sean. "Hey, didn't you guys revamp the firehouse? How's it going?"

"It's great. Really gives us more space and makes the long hours more comfortable…"

He felt a touch on his shoulder and looked up at Angel. "Cal, I heard a motorcycle."

"Yeah, I know. We gotta get used to not reacting every time a cycle goes by, or we'll go nuts."

She knelt down beside him. "Cal, the house is too far from the road to hear a motorcycle passing by."

Shit, of course. His breath quickened. *Get a grip; it's probably nothing.* He listened and very clearly heard a motorcycle outside the house. Maybe a friend of Jake's or Roan's? He couldn't move. Angel was equally still beside him. The conversation went on around them. Sean began talking to Roan; Em came back in and sat beside Jake. Neither Cal nor Angel moved at all.

Then they heard the doorbell.

Jake looked up. "Are we expecting anyone?" He glanced at Cal and Angel. Cal swallowed hard but couldn't get the words out. Jake seemed to pick up the vibe and went immediately toward the entry.

Cal heard voices, one of them soft and a bit high. Angel gripped his hand so tight he figured his blood flow stopped. Who needed blood flow? By this time the rest of the group had noticed their riveted attention and were staring either at Cal and Angel or toward the door.

Jake came around the corner. And there was Eli. Oh sweet God. Eli. He'd come to Thanksgiving. Dressed in jeans, a white shirt, and a wool sport coat. His golden hair was tied at his neck, and that perfect, pink-cheeked face was on display.

Angel let out a squeal that could break glass. She leaped up, raced across the space, and, from a couple of feet away, threw herself at Eli. Good thing the guy was strong, because she was a hurtling missile. He managed to stay upright and catch her as her arms surrounded his neck and her long legs circled his waist. "You're back. You're back." She kissed his forehead and cheeks while he laughed like he'd been attacked by a puppy. Then she stopped kissing and looked steadily into the golden eyes. "You are back, aren't you? Because if you say you're just here for dinner, I will personally poison your food!"

That got a laugh, not only from him, but from the group.

Cal had stood but hadn't moved closer. Eli looked up at him, his gold eyes shining. "Yes. I'm back, if you'll have me. I went yesterday to Global Outreach, and it seems they could really use a guy who can build clinics and houses. So if it's okay, I'll go to Africa with you."

Angel was going nuts. "Hell yeah, it's okay. Think of everything we can do…" She looked back at Cal. "It is okay, isn't it, Cal?"

Cal cocked his head. "Good way to get away from the press and your father, I'd guess, going to Africa."

Eli nodded. "Yes."

Cal couldn't quite catch his breath. "You don't really have to go with us. It's a big continent."

Angel looked between them, then slid herself down Eli's body until she was on her feet. "That's true. You don't have to go with us" -- she looked at him through her lashes -- "if you don't want to."

Eli looked at the two of them and then glanced around the room. There wasn't a sound except the soft gurgle of water from the fountain in the entry. Every gaze was focused on Eli. He put his hands on his hips. "Okay, critter, don't give me that coy bullshit. You're about as demure as a charging rhino. If I said I didn't want to go with you, you'd serve my balls as giblets. And you." He walked the distance to Cal and looked up in his face. "Yes, I know I'm a lousy, traitorous, pain-in-the-ass commitment-phobe, but I'm the pain-in-the-ass that" -- he swallowed hard -- "loves you." He looked down and spoke softly. "Nothing in my life has made sense since I met both of you, and it will never make sense again without you."

"No more running?"

Eli grinned. "Still running, but I'd like to run with you instead of away from you."

Shit, Cal's heart wouldn't stay in his chest. He grabbed Eli by the shoulders, turned him, and pressed their mouths together, then held out an arm and felt Angel walk under it. He raised his head from Eli's and kissed Angel, vaguely aware of the cheering in the background.

Shakti's voice penetrated the pandemonium. "Somebody call in the kids. This is the education of a lifetime."

When Cal stopped kissing Angel, he raised his head to find Shakti standing beside him. "I gather *this* is Elijah." She threw both arms around the man and gave him a huge hug. "I told you I love a man with balls."

Chapter Twenty-three

Cal and Angel lay on the bed while Eli wandered through the guesthouse running his hands over the cabinetry. He called from the living room, "Hey, this room is great. I love how the cabinets work. Jeez, this finish turned out so smooth."

Cal smiled at Angel. "I think we should put his hands to better work, whaddya say?"

"Hell, yes." She scooted out of her jeans, leaving her in a pair of tiny pink thong panties and a sweater. She pulled the top over her head, and since she never wore a bra, the panties were now doing a solo. Cal pulled off his own sweater and unfastened his jeans. He'd been half-hard all afternoon while they had dinner, just thinking about getting fucked by Eli while he fucked Angel. Now the man was admiring cabinets, for crap's sake, and they were dying here.

Cal pulled out his hard-as-nails erection and started stroking. Angel pushed the pink panty crotch aside and stuck a finger in what looked to be one seriously dripping pussy. Oh yeah, the smell of sex rose from both of them.

"Hey, don't you think it was a good choice to go with black lacquer on these cabinets --" Eli came around the corner. "Holy shit!"

Cal pulled his penis hard. "Your Thanksgiving dessert. Just keeping it warm for you."

Eli's pupils dilated until they were all black. "Oh crap, don't stop." He pulled his shirt off and followed with his jeans, then made a dive for the bed. He positioned himself below their two bodies. First, he leaned over to Angel, pushed her hand aside, and stuck as much of his tongue as he could get into her dripping slit.

"Holy merde!" Her hips came off the bed.

Eli's hand groped over toward Cal. Oh yeah, manual dexterity. Cal helped him out by wrapping Eli's fingers around his cock. The hand began pumping while Eli ate her. After a minute, he switched, sticking two fingers into Angel's pussy, and moving over to swallow down Cal's cock. Cal couldn't tell whose hips were working harder, his or Angel's. The heat filled him all the way to his heart.

Cal gasped. "We should make you do this for three days just in penance, but crap, I want you to fuck me so bad."

Eli raised his mouth from Cal's cock and smiled like the Cheshire cat. "I thought you'd never ask."

Cal reached for condoms and lube on the bedside table as Angel positioned herself flat on her back. Cal rolled a condom on his wet cock and positioned himself between her legs. He grinned at her. "Hey, critter."

"Hey, mon grand."

"I love you."

"Love you back."

"Gonna fuck you till you can't see."

"Oh, bebe. You're the man to do it."

He plunged his cock into her and felt rough hands on his ass. He stilled while Eli pushed two slick fingers into his hole and gently stroked. "This what you want, big guy?"

"No, pretty boy, get that cock in me."

"Listen to who's bossy now."

"Just do it."

"With pleasure." One hard push and Cal felt balls slap his ass.

Could he have lived without this for his whole life? He knew the answer. Yes, if the cock hadn't been Eli's. He never wanted another man in him or another woman under him. Oh shit, yes. Yes. This was life as it should be. A three-way love might not be the norm, but for some people, it just worked. He'd seen that for himself watching his brother, Em, and Roan, and now he had that kind of love in his own life. "Oh shit, Eli, I love you so much."

"I love you, baby. I love both of you."

Eli pushed in as Cal pushed back onto his cock; then Cal pushed into Angel as Eli withdrew. Soon they had a perfect rhythm, and Cal felt the heat building in his balls.

Angel gasped and laughed joyfully. "See, Cal, he was a commitment-phobe for one lover. It took two to pin him down."

Cal laughed back. Oh God, he'd come in seconds, this was so good. His pretty boy in his ass, and his cock buried in his beautiful tomboy. They'd been through attraction and deception and arrived at love. Just the way it should be.

Meet Tara Lain

Tara Lain believes in happy ever afters - and magic. Same thing. In fact, she says, she doesn't believe, she knows. Tara shares this passion in her stories that star her unique, charismatic heroes and adventurous heroines. Quarterbacks and cops, werewolves and witches, blue collar or billionaires, Tara's characters, readers say, love deeply, resolve seemingly insurmountable differences, and ultimately live their lives authentically. After many years living in southern California, Tara, her soulmate honey and her soulmate dog decided they wanted less cars and more trees, prompting a move to Ashland, Oregon where Tara's creating new stories and loving living in a small town with big culture. Likely a Gryffindor or maybe a Ravensclaw but possessed of Parseltongue, Tara loves animals of all kinds, diversity, open minds, coconut crunch ice cream from Zoeys, and her readers. She also loves to hear from you.

Visit my website: https://taralain.com/ for a FREE download of my Sample Book.

If you like to stay up to date on books in general and mine in particular, come join my Reader Group on Facebook: HEA, Magic, and Beautiful Boys.

Subscribe to my Newsletter and go into a Draw for fun prizes in every issue.

Follow me on Amazon for all the new releases.

And on Bookbub for specials and to see the books that I love.

Of course, you'll find me on Facebook, Twitter, Pinterest, and Instagram

Books by Tara Lain

Cataclysmic Shift

BALLS TO THE WALL:

Volley Balls • Fire Balls

Beach Balls • FAST Balls

High Balls • Snow Balls • Bleu Balls

Balls to the Wall – Volley Balls and Fire Balls Anthology

Balls to the Wall – Beach Balls and FAST Balls Anthology

Balls to the Wall – High Balls and Snow Balls Anthology

COWBOYS DON'T:

Cowboys Don't Come Out

Cowboys Don't Ride Unicorns

Cowboys Don't Samba

DREAMSPUN BEYOND #15 – Rome and Jules

DREAMSPUN DESIRES #5 – Taylor Maid

LOVE IN LAGUNA:

Knight of Ocean Avenue

Knave of Broken Hearts

Prince of the Playhouse

Lord of a Thousand Steps

Fool of Main Beach

LOVE YOU SO:

Love You So Hard

Love You So Madly

Love You So Special

Love You So Sweetly

A Love You So Anthology – Love You So Hard and Love You So Madly

MIDDLEMARK MYSTERIES:

The Case of the Sexy Shakespearean

The Case of the Voracious Vintner

MOVIE MAGIC ROMANCES:

Return of the Chauffeur's Son

Love and Linguistics

PENNYMAKER TALES:

Sinders and Ash • Driven Snow

Beauty, Inc. • Never

Sinders and Ash and Beauty, Inc. Anthology

SUPERORDINARY SOCIETY:

Hidden Powers

TALES OF THE HARKER PACK:

The Pack or the Panther

Wolf in Gucci Loafers

Winter's Wolf

The Pack or the Panther & Wolf in Gucci Loafers Anthology

From Pride Publishing –

DANGEROUS DANCERS:

Golden Dancer

Death Dancer

Keep Reading for an Excerpt from

GENETIC CELEBRITY

Book Four in the Genetic Attraction Series

Coming Soon to Amazon and KU

* * *

"Oh God, Tommy. Oh God. Oh God. Yes, yes! Mmmmmmmm."

Tommy grinned. "That good?"

"Oh God, *yes*!" Her mouth opened wider and stretched…around his wooden spoon. Her pretty red lips pursed just a bit, and he caught a glimpse of the tip of her tongue. Was he a pervert for wishing those lips were stretched around other parts of him? Hell, the age difference wasn't that great. Ten years. Big deal. Roan, his boss, was thirteen years younger than his wife, Em.

Booky collapsed against the granite counter, clutching her chest. "I think you make this even better than Roan, darling. And I don't say that easily."

He rinsed the spoon in the stainless steel sink. "So stay and have some with me. Roan's supposed to come later."

"Do I dare? That will be the third time this month I've missed Mama's family dinner. She'll kill me and ask questions later."

He fished into the steaming pan and grabbed a sliver of chicken. *Okay, try to resist.* Slowly he walked toward her, step by step, waving the piece of meat in his fingers. "Chicken cacciatooooooore. Peppers, onions, tomatoes. Mmmmmmmm."

She squeezed against the counter, fending him off. "Tommy 'Tick Tock' Riley. You're a home wrecker."

"Capers."

She pressed her arm against her forehead. Booky did drama like nobody else. "Oh God, I love capers."

"*Lots* of capers." He stood in front of her. They were practically eye to eye. It would be nice to tower over her, flex his big alpha-male muscles and watch her swoon. Too bad it wasn't gonna happen in this life. Five feet eight and his cooking were all he had, so he'd better use them. He wafted the morsel under her nose. "Smelllll the goodness."

She followed the movement with her nose like a hypnotized cobra. "Oh, poor Mama." Snap. She grabbed the chicken in her teeth and chewed. Eyes closed, moaning. Hell, he'd like to elicit that reaction with other pleasures.

The big brown eyes opened. "She's going to forget what I look like. I'm such a bad daughter." Dramatic pause. "I'll call her and say I'm eating with you tonight. Again!"

Still chewing, she walked around the island counter that separated the kitchen from the huge open space of the loft. She grabbed her purse from the sectional couch and fished out a phone. He got a wink as she dialed.

It wasn't likely anyone would ever forget what Booky Edelson looked like. Her gleaming black hair fell to her shoulders like a curtain of ebony, and the liquid brown eyes peered out from under straight bangs. Bold features, they called them. A long straight nose and full lips. She was slim but curvy with generous breasts and a round butt. Yeah, if you saw her, you never forgot her. And the in-your-face appearance matched a personality just as big.

Why did he adore her? She was everything he said he was tired of and didn't want to be. Aggressive, ambitious, pushy. Just like his parents. Plus, even though he'd always liked women too, he'd pretty much been with men since he was sixteen. His family *really* hated that. He sighed. It didn't matter anyway because she only loved him for his food.

"Hi, Mama." She listened for a minute. "Yeah, that's why I'm calling. I'm at Roan's, and, uh, he has some things for me to do."

She looked up at him. "Yes, Tick Tock is here."

She didn't say anything for seconds, but she looked like she was trying to get a word in. Mouth open, closed. Open.

"Yes, he's cooking dinner but…"

She shifted and actually seemed to cringe. Booky cringing? Her mama was a force.

"Mama, I have to *work*." She listened. He could hear her mother's voice squawking out of the cell phone. "I'll see you next week. Bye, Mama."

She clicked off. "See what you did?" She adopted her best Jewish-mother voice and struck a pose. "So what would a daughter of mine want to be eating with her 'just friend' instead of coming home for dinner where she might get herself a *makher* for a boyfriend?"

Tommy laughed. "What's that mean? It sounds dangerous."

"It kind of is, but it means a person who makes things happen. A mover and shaker. Mama has this doctor she's been trying to fix me up with for weeks. I keep escaping. She's pissed." She bounded around the island. "Okay, I'll make the salad."

"Hey, I don't want her to be mad at me. If I ever get to meet her, I don't want her to kill me too."

She rinsed the lettuce and stuck it in the lettuce dryer. "Mama doesn't mind me hanging with you. She just wants me spending more time with a good Jewish doctor with marriage on his mind."

A doctor who was thirty-seven instead of twenty-five. A mover and shaker. Just like everyone always wanted him to be. Shit. "Why are you resisting? Don't you want to get married?"

She stopped ripping lettuce and cocked her head. "I've been married." She shrugged. "You know, I kind of think I want something I've never had. Something not written down in Mama's book of marriage." She grinned at him. "That's weird, isn't it?"

He stashed some plates in the warmer. "No, actually. It makes perfect sense. Just like I've always wanted something my family didn't have written down in their book of success."

"Hey, you are a success."

"Not by Riley standards. I should be the head of a corporation, some big CFO, or a congressman at least by now."

"But you've helped make Roan a huge success."

He struck his best Napoleon pose. "Rileys don't do things behind the scenes unless it's assistant to the President of the United States. And the cooking thing? Women's work."

She grabbed her chest. "Then I hope you never listen to your family."

"Trust me, I don't."

She smiled. "I guess we're both mavericks."

"I guess." He grabbed some silverware and started to set the table. The lock on the front door rattled. Good. He put down a third place setting.

Booky glanced up from her salad making. "Roan's here."

"Yep."

Tommy looked toward the doorway across the huge open space. He always loved that first moment seeing Roan. The little gasp, the intake of breath. You never got used to it. They didn't call Roan the most beautiful man alive for nothing.

The door opened.

Yep. There he was. Six feet one of black-haired, green-eyed perfection. World's best boss. "Hi, Roan. Hope you're hungry."

The famous smile flashed across the room. He could light up a city. "Starving. I ate rabbit food for three days in Arizona. Hell, they had so much of my skin showing, I didn't dare develop a lump."

As if he had any.

Booky came around the counter. "Hi, darling. I'm here too. How did the shoot go?"

Roan dropped his garment bag on the couch. "Good. They seemed ecstatic, but give them a call to make sure, okay?"

Tommy smiled. Other supermodels would consider the client lucky to get them. Not Roan. Kind, gentle, self-effacing. Tommy's parents hated that he worked behind the scenes for Roan Black. They said Tommy was hiding his light under a bushel. That Roan got all the fame and renown while Tommy got nothing. It wasn't true. Working with Roan had made Tommy rich, but that was the least that he'd gotten. Roan loved home and family more than anything. And he loved to cook. Tommy had modeled himself, no pun intended, after his boss. He looked down at his thin, muscular arms. Shame he didn't look like him.

Roan pulled off his leather jacket and tossed it on the couch next to his bag.

Tommy pointed to it. "Want me to take your stuff upstairs?"

Roan shook his head. "I wanted to check in with you guys first, but I might just make the trip to Connecticut tonight. I miss the family so bad. I told them I'd be home Friday, but a night early is better."

"How's Baby Girl?"

"Growing like a weed. I don't even like to leave her for a day." He walked over to the counter. "Actually, there's something I want to talk to you both about." He inhaled. "God, that smells divine. Is it chicken cacciatore?"

Tommy laughed and went into the gleaming open kitchen. "Yep, and it's coming right up. On the table in five."

"Great. Let me go change and wash up." He bounded across the room to the huge floating staircase and took the stairs two at a time.

Tommy stirred the chicken dish. It did smell good. He took the plates from the warmer and started dishing penne and chicken.

Booky served up the salad.

He grinned. "Did you use every artichoke heart in the house?"

"You know my weakness for artichokes."

He spooned a caper and held it out to her. "You have many weaknesses, my dear."

"And I'm proud of every one." She breathed in, then opened her mouth, touched the spoon with her tongue, and sucked the caper in.

His cock leaped. He turned away. That woman could turn him on with a smile but when she used her tongue? Jeez. He was sick.

Breathe. He carried the steaming plates to the table, and she followed with the salads.

Her voice was soft. "What do you think Roan wants to talk about?"

"You know what."

She sighed just as Roan came down the stairs. He'd changed out of his dress clothes into jeans and a T-shirt and looked just as beautiful and a lot more comfortable. He crossed to the big table and pulled out his chair on the far side, his back to the floor-to-ceiling windows. He insisted that Tommy sit at the head because he lived in the loft while Roan only visited. Of course, Roan had lived here before he moved to Connecticut, and he owned half the building while Tommy owned the other half, but he didn't acknowledge that. "I'm starved."

They all sat and plunged into the food.

Booky moaned in appreciation. She sounded like she was in the midst of the world's best orgasm, and dammit, he'd missed his part in it.

Roan chewed slowly, eyes closed. The heavy black lashes fanned his high cheekbones. "Tommy, you've outdone yourself."

Booky stopped chewing for a half second. "So tell me about the shoot."

"Great. The new line is fabulous. I loved it."

"Have they picked a shot for the cover?"

"Yeah. It's quite something. Swim trunks and a motorcycle jacket. I was decked out in guyliner and black nail polish. They wove beads in my hair. Not really my style, but I think it turned out okay."

"I'm sure it was great."

They chewed.

Roan shifted in his chair. Yeah, he was fidgety because he knew how much Booky hated the subject about to come up. Tommy took a breath. Poor Booky.

"Uh, I was working with two other guys and a couple girls. I felt ancient. One of the girls was fourteen. The oldest guy was nineteen."

She set down her fork. This was an appetite spoiler for sure. "Roan. You're twenty-five. Not exactly middle-aged."

"You know as well as I do that in modeling twenty-five is ancient. Plus, I may be kind of androgynous, but compared to some of these guys I'm an alpha male." He folded his napkin beside his plate. Well hell. He'd only eaten half his food. "Booky, I don't need the money. I know it's hard to let go, but I want to spend more time with my family. Jake and Em work so hard at the lab. I can do most of my real estate work and manage my cosmetic brand from home with Tommy handling a lot of the heavy lifting. That way I can be with Baby Girl so she doesn't grow up thinking the nanny is one of her parents. I need to retire and let whoever comes up be the next big thing."

"But that's the problem. There is no next big thing." She got up and paced toward the kitchen, then turned. "Roan, you're the biggest male supermodel of all time. You can't fill that void with just anybody."

Yeah, and Roan was her biggest client. Tommy didn't think that Booky needed money too much either. Hell, if she ever did, he'd love to support her. But she was the Booky. She had made Roan the biggest thing since…well, since anybody. Nobody had ever done it before with a male model. She'd nurtured his career like a hothouse orchid, and now he wanted to walk away. Poor Booky.

Roan shook his head. "I'm not that irreplaceable."

"Ask any client, Roan. They'll tell you how irreplaceable you are."

He sighed and pushed back his chair. "The fact remains that I want to retire. I don't want you to leave me. I want you to keep working. Maybe I'll lecture or do appearances or something." Tommy knew he was clutching at straws to keep Booky happy. Roan wanted to stay home. Period. From the bottom of his heart, Tommy understood it.

Roan got up from the table and walked into the main living area. Tommy watched the slump of those beautiful broad shoulders. Roan put on his leather jacket and picked up his bag. He didn't even turn. "Sorry, guys. I'm tired. I'm going home."

He walked to the door and left.

Tommy felt Booky vibrating beside him. "Oh God, what did I do?" She grabbed his arm. "You have to stop me when I do shit like that to Roan. Please, Tommy. He's one of the best people I've ever known. He doesn't deserve my drama."

"He understands, Booky. It's your career too."

"I know, but I don't want to care about that. I want to want the best for him no matter what. I want to." He looked into the bold and beautiful face. Tears ran down her cheeks. "Oh God, I'm such a selfish bitch." She wiped her cheeks with the back of her hand. "It was a great dinner. I'm sorry I wrecked it. I'm going to go home to Mama and try to make it up to her for not coming tonight." She leaned over and kissed his cheek. "Thanks, Tick Tock. I'll see you Monday. Sorry I'm not helping clean up, but I have to get the train to Brooklyn."

She hurried over to the chair near the door where she'd left her jacket and briefcase, looking like if she just got to Brooklyn fast enough, she could find the antidote for bitchiness.

Click. The door closed behind her.

Yep. Here they were again. Just him and the dirty dishes.

He picked up the plates and carried them to the kitchen. His pocket buzzed. About the closest thing to sex he was gonna get tonight.

He looked at the phone. "Shit."

Click. "Hi, Mom."

"Hi, Tommy." She sounded hesitant. Like maybe his lack of ambition was catching. "Uh, you know that your father's birthday party is in three weeks. You will come, won't you? It would make your father so happy."

They both knew that was a lie. His father, the senator, couldn't care less if he was there. But it would look good to the press if all three Riley sons were on hand for the occasion. He wanted so badly to say no, but that was making more of a statement of his black-sheepness than was necessary. "Okay. I'll come."

"That's wonderful, dear. Black-tie and, uh, you can bring a date if you want."

He grinned. It would serve them right if he brought a guy. "Thanks. Maybe I will."

Did he hear her swallow? *Good. Sweat.* "Bye, Mom."